A deadly volley chewed at the barracks near Bolan

The Executioner responded in kind. He fired the PPS 41 subgun from his hip. A stream of 7.62mm rounds ripped into the exposed enemy.

But what Bolan saw as he stepped out from cover spelled big trouble.

Two of the surviving enemy were armed with AK-47s. Others were crouched with grenades in their fists, about to pull the pins.

"Hold your fire!" Bolan yelled. "Don't shoot me!" The enemy did not reply. Nor did they lob the grenades. Bolan had bought a few seconds.

"I'm going to throw out my gun," he called. *"I surrender!"*

MACK

THE EXECUTIONER 54

BOLAN

Mountain Rampage

A GOLD EAGLE BOOK FROM
W RLDWIDE

TORONTO · NEW YORK · LONDON · PARIS
AMSTERDAM · STOCKHOLM · HAMBURG
ATHENS · MILAN · TOKYO · SYDNEY

Dedicated to the quest of Lynn Standerwick.
25, who is seeking her fighter-pilot father.
He was last seen parachuting from his crippled
F-4 over Laos in 1971. Lynn joined former
Green Beret Lt. Col. James "Bo" Gritz in his
secret invasion of Indochina to rescue her
father and other unaccounted-for Americans
who the U.S. government insists are dead.
The mission was unsuccessful, but Lynn can
proudly be ranked among Those Who Dare.

———————————◆◆◆———————————

First edition June 1983

ISBN 0-373-61054-8

Special thanks and acknowledgment to
E. Richard Churchill for his contributions to this work.

Printed in Canada

PROLOGUE

COLORADO STATE TROOPER Larry Bennett drove off the main highway. Once on the winding, less traveled mountain road he reduced his speed. It was the sort of morning more suited to spotting mule deer than to writing citations.

The trooper's eye was drawn to a pair of cars parked on the opposite side of the road ahead of him. A man wearing shorts and sports shirt waved frantically to attract the trooper's attention.

Bennett hit both lights and siren.

He twisted the cruiser in a tight U-turn to pull in behind the halted cars.

"Thank God you're here." The man let the words pour out before Bennett could leave his cruiser. "Fred—he's my brother-in-law—he damned near ran a guy down. We were driving along the road—Fred was in front of me—when this guy comes busting out of the woods and into the road. Fred turned his Ford sideways to avoid him. I almost got the guy with my right fender.''

Bennett held up his hand. "Easy," he said. "Just slow down a bit." He moved toward the knot of people clustered at the highway's edge.

"He's wearing pretty good clothing but it's all torn it up," the man went on. "I think he's spaced out on drugs. He keeps yelling about robots and people running into walls till they die. Must be one hell of a bad trip."

Bennett saw the man huddled on the roadside. He noted with disgust that spittle sprayed from the guy's lips as he shook his head from side to side. Bloody saliva dribbled down his chin from a tongue that had been chewed. Angry red grooves scored his cheeks.

At first Bennett blamed tree branches for the marks. Then he realized the man had clawed his own face in his torment.

But it was his eyes that most affected the trooper. Wild, crazed, darting, they were filled with terror.

A pretty woman, about Bennett's age, looked at the trooper. In her hand she held a handkerchief stained with the bloody froth she had cleaned from the man's chin and throat.

"He's afraid of wolves," she said. "He keeps telling us about wolves eating people." Her eyes showed deep concern for the tormented man on the gravel beside her. Calm serenity shone from her features. Just like Bennett's nurse in Nam.

The trooper froze. Nam. The man's eyes, his disjointed attempts to communicate. He was like the corporal in the bed beside Bennett in the field hospital, the guy a patrol picked up after the VC had played their games with him.

"He's not on drugs," the trooper said. "Help me get him into the cruiser."

"Shouldn't he have an ambulance?" the woman asked.

"No time. He's dying. Give me a hand."

Minutes later, Larry Bennett was pushing the white cruiser through turns, driving with one hand as he clutched the mike with the other to issue frantic requests. The dispatcher, no stranger to mountain tragedy, relayed Bennett's needs without comment.

"It's the lost hiker we got the missing report on last Monday," Bennett concluded.

"Wrong location. You're forty miles too far north," came the reply.

"Believe me. It's the same guy. How many hikers have custom boots with the right heel built up an extra inch and a half? It's the same guy."

Then he was gunning down the highway with both hands on the wheel, his lights and siren giving him the driving room.

It was Nam again. Bennett began to pray to the God of all tormented men everywhere.

In the cruiser's rear seat, a man wrestled with inner terrors and, with darting eyes, watched for the wolves he knew lurked close by.

MINUTES SHORT OF TWO that afternoon, Trooper Bennett's radio came to life.

"That guy you delivered to the hospital this morning."

"Right."

"He died about half an hour ago. Thought you'd want to know."

1

Mack Bolan halted in mid-stride. The big warrior's keen senses warned him he was no longer alone. On all sides were the rocks and broken forest of Colorado's high country. A mile ahead lay the target of his soft probe. Seven rugged mountain miles behind him was the site where Jack Grimaldi, flying a military chopper, had dropped the big man just after sunrise.

"Stay hard, Sarge," Grimaldi had said, repeating their customary parting words.

Bolan had raised a loose fist, thumb extended toward the sky. Then, without a backward glance, he moved from the drop site toward the hellground that awaited him.

Bolan now stood motionless. In battle black, he blended into the tree-cast shadows. He heard the sound of a boot scuffing on stone. At more than ten thousand feet above sea level, in the rarefied air, far from the noise of city and civilization, sounds carried, sights and smells were clearer.

Moving only his head, the Executioner faced toward the sound's source. A figure three hundred yards away caught his attention. A second figure came briefly into view before vanishing into a stand of lodgepole pines. Three greyhounds ranged ahead of the pair.

Bolan, on higher ground, knew he was safe from discovery by the dogs because the morning breeze was rising along the mountain slopes.

Satisfied that the rifle-toting pair were not an immediate problem, Bolan took his 10x50 binoculars from their case, moved silently a half-dozen yards before resting his elbows on a rock outcrop, and began a careful survey of the area between him and the site of his soft probe.

Bolan was no stranger to Colorado. During his earlier self-declared war on the Mafia he had visited the Centennial State long enough to let Colorado's crime lords know they were not beyond the Executioner's reach. By the time he had left Colorado he had made his point. In spades.

Now the big guy was back. The ramblings

of a tormented hiker had set things in motion. That, along with an almost incredible rumor, had brought Bolan to the Colorado high country.

His eyes swept the open valley. Nothing about the peaceful scene suggested it was the site of experiments aimed at the control of a nation's people. Nothing, that is, except a dying man's screams and maybe a couple of hundred missing people.

Satisfied that the actual site matched the mental image he had formed from the aerial photos and survey maps, Bolan returned his attention to the pair and their dogs. The glasses brought them into focus whenever they appeared between the trees. Booted, jean-clad, both wore denim jackets. One wore a battered felt hat with a low crown and wide brim while the other, in command of the dogs, was bareheaded.

For the moment Bolan gave his attention to the second person. Slim, moving with grace, she had long golden hair that fell almost to the middle of her back. For the second time in half a minute she halted.

Bolan looked at her older, weathered partner. The man gestured with his rifle. The woman came to his side. Slowly the two continued, their path taking them farther from Bolan.

They were tracking something.

Again Bolan's battle senses brought him to full alert. He let the Bausch & Lomb binoculars hang from their leather thong as he brought his M-1 with its Smith & Wesson scope into position. Below him, a third figure came into view. Seconds later, another stalker appeared fifty yards to that man's right.

Both men wore combat boots shined to a dull luster; their tailored fatigues were creased, starched and immaculate, and they wore boxed fatigue hats. Right, one question answered. The area was patrolled. And from the looks of the pair, the patrol was professional.

The old man and the woman and their dogs were unaware that now *they* were being followed. Slowly they tracked whatever spoor drew them on. The trio of greyhounds ranged ahead, unaware of any danger.

With practiced fingers, Bolan took inventory of the tools and weapons of war he carried. Spare clips and ammo for the AutoMag and the 9mm silenced Beretta nestled securely in their usual places.

The big silver .44 AutoMag with its full

load of 240-grain messengers of death hung low on one hip. The Beretta 93-R was on the other, in its special holster, ready to deal whispered death. Grenades, plastique in waxed paper wrapping, electronic detonators and a radio-control sender were in place on his webbing, along with the medical field kit and insulated carbon-steel wire cutters. The combat gear was completed with a pair of piano-wire garrotes, and a thin stiletto with twin edges that put a razor to shame.

He was ready. As ready as he would ever be.

You prepared as well as you could and tried to cover every possible angle. But you knew you could never foresee all the problems. Play it by ear. Use past experience as a base. Evaluate every situation as it unfolds. Take no stupid chances but remain willing to live to the limit. Yes, and even beyond. That was all a man could do.

With skills honed razor sharp during his two previous wars, in Vietnam and in America, the warrior moved forward. Bolan was well aware his soft probe could turn hard in a single heartbeat.

Ahead, the drama he anticipated was played out with savage intensity. The pair in battle dress closed in on the old man and the woman. A command cut through the mountain air.

The man, woman and their three greyhounds turned, taken by surprise. One of the autocarbines erupted, sending a hail of whining .22 sizzlers ripping into the dogs.

Bolan's eyes iced over at the brutality. His mind stored the fact that only one of the two on patrol fired—his fire accurate and devastating.

The other man covered the hunter and woman with easy confidence. If these two indicated the capability of the men guarding the secluded hardsite that was Bolan's goal, his mission would not be easy. But he was committed to it, and that meant he had to hold back now.

At a spoken command, the captured pair glanced at each other. They lowered their rifles to the ground, then stepped back. From his vantage point, Bolan saw the man stare steadily at his captors. The woman's attention was on her savaged greyhounds.

One of the patrolling pair stepped forward, closing the distance between himself and the captives. His words were too quiet for Bolan to hear. The old man's head rose, his shoulders squared.

In the blinking of an eye, the barrel of the autocarbine slashed across the short space between the two. The old man staggered from the force of the blow to the side of his head. But he did not go down. He pulled himself erect. Deliberately he reset his hat.

The woman stepped forward to intervene. The second of the pair of uniformed men closed in on her. The barrel of his weapon drove deep into her belly. Even as she sagged forward, hands clawing for the barrel, the man in fatigues reversed the weapon. In an easy, practiced move, he slammed the butt into the small of her back.

Bolan's jaw hardened as the woman sank to the ground. Her companion moved to assist her, but a carbine barrel blocked his way. Without a glance in the direction of the man who had just pistol-whipped him, the old fellow brushed the barrel aside. The sweep of his hand said it all. Fearless for his own safety, the old guy showed nothing but contempt for the pair in their spotless uniforms.

With his back turned to the two, the old man in the worn blue jacket helped the woman to her feet. For seconds she clung to him. Then slowly, deliberately, she straightened. Bolan knew what it cost her to do so. He also knew the physical effort and sheer will it took for the woman to let her hands hang free at her sides.

Another command was given. Neither captive gave evidence of having heard. An auto-carbine's barrel prodded the woman's bruised kidneys. The old man, protecting her, pulled her back.

One of the patrolling pair gathered the rifles while his partner gestured the captives ahead with a motion of his weapon. The silent parade made its way slowly toward lower ground where the open valley floor nestled at slightly less than ten thousand feet.

The captives walked close to each other. From time to time the old man reached out to touch the woman. It was a comforting gesture. The woman walked with her head high, back straight, her every movement full of defiance.

Once certain of the path the group was taking, Mack Bolan set his own course parallel to theirs.

Minutes later, Bolan halted just short of the wooded area. Ahead, a third man in fatigues leaned against the back of a Jeep CJ-5. Conversation drifted to Bolan. Though the words were indistinct, the meaning was clear. The two captives were directed to a point a dozen yards from the CJ-5 and told to sit on the ground. After handcuffing the man's wrist to the woman's ankle, the patrol members gathered at the front of the vehicle.

The three hardguys were evidently used to having things go their way. Mission accomplished, they were relaxing.

Between Bolan and the CJ-5 a rock outcrop loomed. Without hesitation, using the outcrop for cover, the big guy left the sheltering trees and crossed the open space, reaching the rocky protection.

Silently he left the M-1 and its night scope leaning against the boulder. Then he rounded the outcrop and began crossing the thirty or so yards that remained between him and the CJ-5.

Three pairs of hard eyes watched him.

"Hi," Bolan said. The guns holstered at his waist were clearly visible as he stepped forward.

Bolan was moving in for a closer look here. He needed some information. He would give them just enough time to provide it before his soft probe turned hard.

"I seem to have lost my way."

One of the three, the hardguy who had remained at the Jeep, slipped a weapon from the driver's seat and approached Bolan. He carried the Remington 1100 Magnum autoloader with casual confidence.

Behind him, the other two took up positions on either side of the CJ-5.

Bolan noted the weapons the pair carried. As he had suspected, they were American Arms 180 autocarbines. The circular magazine that topped each gun held one hundred seventy-seven lethal .22 long-rifle zingers when the magazine was full to capacity. Three mutilated greyhound bodies had absorbed a portion of the hot lead from one magazine.

Bolan knew both weapons were of the selective-fire variety, supposedly restricted to use by law-enforcement officers. And he knew both weapons were ready to spew their deadly little sizzlers into his body at the touch of eager fingers.

"You're lost all right, buddy." The muzzle of the autoloading Remington 12-gauge lifted in a silent threat.

So much for the outside chance that the hardsite was less sinister than intel had led Stony Man to believe.

These men's weaponry and their spit-and-polish appearance bespoke training and professionalism. The Laser-Lok beam sights on the autocarbines were not necessary for an informal roadblock established to keep the curious out of a secluded mountain retreat. Armed killer patrols were not necessary to secure the perimeter of a harmless hideaway.

"I wonder if you can help me get straightened out?" Bolan asked. The warrior in black was narrowing the distance between himself and the cold-eyed trio.

"We'll be happy to straighten you out," said the dog killer on the far side of the CJ-5.

Bolan continued to advance slowly, steadily. He had seen enough.

"I've got a map here a buddy drew for me," he said. Bolan glanced down as though to locate the map in one of his many slit pockets.

The downward glance was as telling as Bolan knew it would be: no gunman in his right mind would look away from his target while clawing for his weapon. "I'm hunting for Wolf Mountain."

Bolan's big hand moved faster than the eye could follow. Instead of the promised map, the Beretta filled his fist.

The point man heard the word "mountain" and nothing more. A red eye appeared in the center of his forehead.

The 9mm jacketed parabellum slug plowed through the hardguy's brain as though it did not exist. The slug exited through the back of the skull. A chunk of bone and scalp the size of a small child's hand departed with it.

The Beretta again whispered its silent tune. The guy on the near side of the Jeep took a slug that ripped through his larynx. A good portion of his throat exited with the slug. Crimson spurted from the torn flesh. Realization struck as a fountain of red gushed onto the front of his fatigues. His eyes widened. Dying, but not accepting the fact, the hardman was swinging up his 180 carbine. Another slug crashed into his breastbone, throwing him back against the side of the CJ-5. His torn body crumpled down the side of the vehicle to the dust at his booted feet.

Two down. One in the wings.

Bolan's lightning reflexes had already turned the machine pistol toward the guy on the far side of the Jeep. His only concern was for the two captives on the ground behind his target.

As the Executioner squeezed off his fourth single-shot round, the guard's finger was caressing the trigger of the 180. The air was suddenly full of whining .22 muzzle issue, any one of which could tear a fatal chunk from Bolan's head.

Bolan snapped a fifth round off as his previous jacketed slug tore out the back of the man's left shoulder.

The new round cored dead center into the guy's chest. He staggered slightly, the metal punching through his lungs and blasting out of an exit hole large enough to contain a grapefruit.

But the guy's finger never slackened its pressure on the trigger of the autocarbine. Like angry hornets released from captivity, the little .22 hummers filled the air above the Executioner. Bolan dropped to the ground.

Then the chattering carbine ceased its talk of death. The man lay on the ground, his weapon still within the grasp of his hand. Bolan saw fingers twitch spasmodically, become still, twitch again.

Wary, Bolan approached the fallen guard. Their eyes met. Dull, full of the awareness of dying, the man's eyes were nevertheless those of a soldier. A guy would rather have this type on his own side; there was a professional edge to those whose souls die even before recruitment—they have that much less to lose, but they hold onto it twice as viciously.

As Bolan watched, the eyes became sightless and life left. Bolan eased the dead guy's weapon free of slack fingers, then deftly released the partially spent magazine before tossing the weapon into the rear of the Jeep.

So much for the soft probe.

2

"PRETTY FAIR SHOOTING," said the grizzled old man, who sat with his knees drawn up, his wrist bound securely to the slim ankle of the woman at his side.

She sat with her arms behind her, supporting her upper body. Her bootless foot extended forward, held prisoner by the stainless-steel handcuff. Her calm gray eyes regarded Bolan.

"Think you might be in a position to do something about this?" the old man asked, rattling the short chain joining the two.

"Which one has the key?" Bolan asked.

"None of them, if they can be believed," said the old man as he spat a stream of brown tobacco juice onto a small stone. "Said the key was down at the main house." He gestured with his head in the direction of the compound.

"I'm Josh Williams, and this is my grandkid, Sara.'' The sun highlighted the graying stubble on his chin.

"I'm John Phoenix,'' Bolan said.

Sara continued to stare at the warrior, but she made no effort to join the conversation.

"Think maybe you might shoot that chain in two?''

Bolan slipped the small carbon-steel wire cutters from his belt and gestured with their tip. Josh lifted his hand, bringing Sara's foot with it. Bolan positioned the cutters and brought his strength to bear on the handles. Twin cutting edges bit into the hardened steel chain, then snapped it. The old man's hand jerked free and the girl's ankle pulled away.

The warrior extended his free hand and helped Josh up. Bolan studied the cuff on the old man's wrist and used the carbon-steel cutters again. Josh pressed with his free hand against the opposite side of the cuff to give Bolan as much distance as possible between cutting blades and flesh. Bolan brought the two handles together with steady pressure. The blade tips connected, and Josh Williams was free of the stainless-steel cuff.

"Your turn,'' Bolan said, looking at the woman.

She stared at him. "Do you always carry

cutters with insulated handles every time you get lost in the mountains?'' she asked.

"When I know I'm going to need them," Bolan said.

Even with Sara pressing against the lower side of the cuff as hard as she could, there was little space between stainless steel and tender flesh.

"I may nick you," Bolan cautioned.

The tip of the cutting blades bit into her as the blades met. Blood stained her white sock. She did not flinch.

"We're much obliged to you, Mr. Phoenix," Josh said.

Bolan stood and slipped the carbon-steel cutters into their slim sheath before turning to confront Josh. The old man held his rifle with the muzzle pointed near Bolan.

"Those Remington 700 Classics are real pretty," Bolan said. "That adjustable sliding rear ramp-sight makes it a good high-country weapon. Chambered for .270?"

"That's right." The old man studied Bolan closely.

"You using the 150-grain slug?" Bolan asked.

"Nope. I'm shooting 130s. They give a bit more bullet speed."

"About 3,140 feet per second," Bolan smiled.

"About." Josh looked away from him. "Mr. Phoenix knows his guns," he told his granddaughter.

"I heard." She was standing now, both boots on. She walked off to retrieve her own rifle.

Bolan studied her. Her body was slim, lithe, yet richly curved. It suggested great inner strength. Twenty-four or -five, he guessed. Her hair fell in a cascade of rich color in the bright sunlight. She was taller than average but not lanky. Her voice was warm, rich, womanly.

Around her neck, on a braided lanyard, was a whistle for the dogs. Her hands and fingers were long, slim, tapering. Musician's hands. Hands ready to coax a symphony of death from the Winchester 70 STR she was pointing at Bolan. He knew her casual stance for what it was, the competence of someone ready and willing to trigger a shot into him or anyone else, should the need arise.

"Your granddaughter like that little .243?" Bolan asked Josh.

The old man nodded. From inside a mass of leathery wrinkles his pale blue eyes peered brightly. Something seemed to amuse him. "For a city dude you're about half bright."

Bolan pointed to the three fallen men. "Them? Are they city dudes?"

Josh shot a second stream of brown juice in the general direction of the distant compound. "They're parasites."

"You should know," Sara said to Bolan.

She turned on the worn heel of her boot and approached the Jeep. From its rear rack she extracted a shovel. Rifle in her right hand, the tool in her left, she started back up the slope.

"Going to bury her dogs," Josh said. He squatted, his rifle now pointed ninety degrees away from Bolan.

The man in black stood easy, his icy eyes and keen senses constantly alert.

"You government?" Josh demanded at last.

"In a way. Not the sort of government you've run into in the past."

The old man took in the combat scene around them. He spoke wearily.

"We were out after coyotes this morning. I run a deeded ranch near here and rent government graze during the summer. Until this weirdo outfit bought in and started building, we never had much trouble with coyotes. Last few months the blasted critters have been everywhere.''

Bolan heard the distant sound of a truck engine. It came from far south of them. He said nothing.

''Thought we'd see if we could get a line on them with the dogs. Maybe even the odds a bit. Greyhounds are about the only dogs around that are any good against coyotes. Don't know what we'll use now.'' Again a stream of brown juice punctuated his words.

''Other than coyotes, what—who were you tracking?'' Bolan asked.

Josh rose slowly to his feet. He stared to the south. ''Truck's bringing in supplies,'' he said. ''Same time every day.''

Bolan let the conversation lapse.

''You know what parasites are?'' the old man asked at last.

Bolan nodded.

''You know what they call this place?'' He gestured to the unseen compound with his head. ''State and county records say it's the Paradise Valley Rest Home. Some rest home that runs armed patrols! They trying to keep the resters in or us out?''

The sound of the truck was stilled. Another lighter engine was firing up.

"How many patrol units do they have?" Bolan asked.

"One out at all times. One, maybe two, on roving patrol. This one—" he jerked his head at the CJ-5 beside them "—was a rover. We didn't expect it."

Josh glanced at the level of the sun overhead. He decided to open up.

"Sara wanted to be a nurse. She wanted it bad ever since her parents were killed in a head-on crash with a drunk and I took up raising her. So Sara went to university, got qualified and went to work down toward Denver. She was happy as a girl could be.

"She was working the night shift in surgical recovery. One night a pair of dope addicts came looking for drugs. They grabbed a student nurse and started saying what they would do to her if Sara didn't get the drugs they wanted. She got them the drugs and a little something extra. Sara was always sort of quick with her hands. She picked up a scalpel when she went for the drugs. My little grandkid gave more than drugs to that pair. She got them good.

"The next day she came back home, back

to the mountains. She decided to apply for nursing work at Paradise Valley.'' Josh paused and listened.

The vehicle was coming closer but did not pose an immediate threat. Even so, Bolan unleathered the 93-R and moved the fire-selector lever with his right thumb to the three white dots that indicated burst fire.

''But Sara didn't get a nursing job,'' Bolan finished when the old man remained silent.

''Right. She said the place was more like a prison than a rest home.'' Josh's washed-out blue eyes met the icy blue ones of the younger warrior. ''We were tracking a young fella named Doug Fletcher today, that's what we were doing. Doug neighbors to the east of us. Took it into his head that he wanted to check up on this place. That was three days ago.''

The radio in the CJ-5 came to life in a crackle of sound. No more than half a mile away the approaching vehicle geared down, its engine changing pitch as it took the strain of a steep grade.

''Sara and I best be on our way,'' the old man said. ''We're situated due north on the other side of that ridge. Sign over the cattle guard says Rocking JW. That's us. Just don't come in too quiet. Let us know you're about.''

Josh turned to go, paused to rub his bruised head, then turned back. From his jacket pocket he withdrew a plug of tobacco and bit a chunk from it. He offered the plug to Bolan.

"I don't use it, but thanks."

The old man nodded, then he set out up the slope to join the young woman.

The oncoming vehicle's engine changed pitch again as the driver shifted. Bolan moved quickly toward an outcrop he had already decided was his best position both defensively and offensively. He detoured to retrieve his M-1.

As he awaited the unfolding of events, Bolan reflected on the scene just passed. It is possible to know a man for years, to work with him and fight beside him and yet never to become friends with him. Or, you might meet a man, talk with him and become friends immediately. Josh's acceptance of Bolan meant much to the big guy. The old man had fiber—and so did his granddaughter.

Given a dozen like them, Bolan could whip a whole army.

3

APRIL ROSE GLANCED UP as Herman "Gadgets" Schwarz entered the War Room.

"Grimaldi is waiting it out at Fort Carson, just outside of Colorado Springs. He'll be ready when Striker gives him the word."

Stony Man Farm, in the Blue Ridge Mountains, was suddenly so far from where April wanted to be. She twisted the pencil she held, became conscious of what she was doing, then laid it aside.

Though he did not take part in the brief interchange, Aaron "The Bear" Kurtzman was aware of every word spoken. Face drawn, showing strain, the computer genius did not look up from his console screen. His tobacco-stained fingers played a tune that only he understood as they danced across the console's keys. "Check the master video screen," he said without turning away from the console. "I've got some new stuff coming in."

An aerial photo appeared before them.

"This and the ones following were taken during a flyover earlier this morning by a USAF jet."

All eyes focused on the photo. The Bear punched a key. A new photo appeared, bright on the huge video screen.

The Paradise Valley Rest Home was visible in perfect detail. The trio studied the newly arrived photo. April eventually broke the silence.

"Nothing we didn't already have. Signs of recent construction. A real-lock fence around the entire area. It looks very professionally laid out."

Another photo appeared on the screen. The infrared photography brought night-hidden images to light.

"These were taken this morning about three, Mountain Daylight Time," Kurtzman reported.

In slow procession a series of photos came to life on the big screen.

"Freeze that one!" April said.

The image remained before them. Details sharpened as Aaron fiddled briefly with his controls.

"Look at those animals. There must be a

hundred or more. What are they? Dogs?''
she asked.

"Not dogs," Kurtzman said. "Coyotes."

"A hundred fifty coyotes all in one
place?" muttered Gadgets.

No one had an answer, all remained silent,
surveying the photo.

"It has to be food," April said at last.
"Only food would bring so many coyotes to
one place."

She turned to the others.

"Why weren't these photos available to us
sooner?" she asked. "Mack should have
known about this."

Aaron shrugged. "Delay in transmission,
April. Someone along the line was slow, got
tied up, didn't understand the importance of
what he had. It happens."

Sure, things like that happen all the time.
Again she gave her attention to the mill-
ing mass of coyotes on the screen. A shud-
der ran the length of her spine. She glanced
at the two men, managed to control her
anger.

Then, as though drawn to it, April viewed
the screen once more. What sort of
hellground was Mack about to enter this
time?

AGAIN THE APPROACHING VEHICLE changed gears. Bolan's trained ears kept track of its speed.

Yeah, professionals. The downshift meant one, perhaps two hardguys had left the vehicle and were now on foot, seeking to flank him. The enemy's strategy brought no change in Bolan's position. First things first.

Between the big guy's protective barrier of rock and the near edge of the forested slopes, the CJ-5 suddenly barrelled through, the driver's foot down hard. To the driver's right sat an alert patrol member armed with an autocarbine. The Jeep's back seat held another man and weapon.

Mack Bolan set his sights on passenger number one. His forefinger caressed the trigger, the M-1 bucked slightly into his broad shoulder, and the guard riding in the front of the Jeep stopped living. A crimson flower of death adorned the left breast pocket of his otherwise spotless fatigues.

As the driver began to react, Bolan lined up the M-1 on the vehicle's back-seat passenger. Even with the Jeep's speed, the shot was routine for the big guy. Just enough lead, a gentle, firm stroke of the trigger.

The slug quartered off the man's breastbone, plowed its way through flesh and muscle and emerged just beneath the left shoulder blade.

Bolan turned his attention to the driver. The guy was spinning the Jeep's steering wheel in a frantic effort to put space between himself and his executioner. Miniature geysers of earth sprayed from the vehicle's four mudgrip tires. The CJ was in a power slide, each tire tearing into the fragile turf beneath its skidding treads.

With one hand the hardguy clawed for the 12-gauge Remington Autoloader racked at his side. Professional to the end, unwilling to face the fact that his luck was gone, the guy was aiming to kill.

The Executioner gently triggered his third round. It lifted the top of the driver's skull from his head. Bits of gray tinged with red decorated the vehicle's windshield. The husk of what had been a man steered the vehicle into a pair of eight-inch-thick lodgepole pines at full throttle.

The numbers were falling fast now. Bolan discarded his M-1 and its night sight and filled his fist with the familiar bulk of Big Thunder. A quick one-eighty gave the big guy a new field of vision.

Twenty-five yards from where he crouched, he saw the business end of an autocarbine appearing around the edge of a rock.

Bolan considered his options, his mind sorting and filing possible courses of action. He wanted some hard intelligence about the compound. Taking this hardguy captive posed no problem that Bolan could not handle. But, putting himself into the minds of those who engineered the area's defense, why drop just one flanker onto the field of battle? Two could have stepped from the CJ as easily as one.

The blitzing warrior went with the odds. By doing so, he issued a death warrant on the guy poking his head around the protective jut of rock.

The .44 AutoMag roared twice. The second shot followed the first so quickly, the open mountain valley below returned only one booming echo. The first 240-grain missile tore the lower jaw free of the man's face. White upper teeth were suddenly revealed. The second mangling messenger of death had entered his head just below the socket of the left eye.

The Executioner was already in motion. If he was wrong about a second killer stalking him on foot, then he was going to be doing some rapid and unnecessary footwork. If he was right, he was in the process of saving his life. Bolan broke from cover, reached the corpse even before it had completed its sag to the ground, and rounded the outcrop of rock at full speed. His right hand full of ready .44 AutoMag, the big guy knew in an instant that his conclusion was correct. Rounding the opposite end of the rocky outgrowth was the fifth member of the team. Looking the other way, the heavily built guy in the snappy fatigues had only one thing in mind—to catch an unsuspecting Bolan and tear his body to shreds with a hail of .22 long-rifle bullets.

Sure, it was a good plan. It was excellent. Only one thing was wrong with it. And that thing now stalked him, with the grace and agility of a jungle cat.

Bolan's target was well trained. What he lacked was the ability to think on his own, to analyze a field situation and improvise if necessary. The big guy closed to within ten yards, and the man he stalked never turned once to glance back over his shoulder.

The big AutoMag with its silver barrel was ready and anxious to thunder death. Then Bolan spoke.

"Twitch once and you die."

The words broke the mountain stillness. For a dozen heartbeats the guy remained immobile.

Gently, as though expecting a burst of whining slugs to rip into his broad back, the man redistributed his weight from one leg to another.

"Drop the gun and turn around slowly," Bolan ordered. His voice had taken on an edge that could cut glass.

The carbine slipped from reluctant fingers. "I'm turning around now. Don't shoot."

Bolan detected a trace of an accent in the man's perfectly enunciated words. European. Perhaps German.

The two big men faced each other. Broader than Bolan, lacking two inches in height, the spit-and-polish patrol member let his eyes travel the length of the blacksuited man before coming to rest on the big .44 that was trained on his thick chest.

"The others all dead?" He knew the answer before framing the question.

Bolan nodded.

"You killed all four that just came up?"

Bolan's expression did nothing to counter the bleak cold of his icy eyes.

His captive shrugged. An insincere smile

softened the lines of his face, relaxed his heavy jaw. He spread both thick-fingered hands in a gesture of defeat. When his palms returned inward, Bolan noted the man's right hand was fractionally nearer the .357 Combat Magnum that hung from his belt.

"Why are men like you hired to patrol a rest home?"

"People with money regard their privacy highly."

"Where is your home in Germany?"

There was a pause. The guy was clearly startled. Then he relaxed.

"Stuttgart." His smile had become a sneer.

"Why would you come all the way from West Germany to help patrol a rest home?"

"Old people need peace and security in which to relax and be restored to health," the guy quoted like a parrot.

"Why are there so many coyotes here suddenly? What brings them?"

"Dogs. The patients have lots of dogs. Not coyotes."

"Why don't you and I just march down there and look around? I'll let you lead the way in case my reception isn't a warm one."

The guy's eyes lifted from Bolan and focused on a point just over his left shoulder.

"See, I told you they were just dogs. Here come some now." His left hand rose with the thick index finger extended.

Fear of being marched captive into the compound outweighed the man's fear of the black-clad warrior and his big .44 AutoMag. The man's timing was excellent. As he lifted his left arm, he dropped his right hand onto the butt of the .357. Had Bolan turned his head as the guard hoped, the ruse would have succeeded. The only flaw in the plan was the combat quality of Mack Bolan.

Bolan's 240-grain slammer tore through the center of the guy's throat. It ripped its way out the back of the broad neck carrying chunks of vertebrae. As the thick body began to sag, the guy's large head lolled grotesquely onto one shoulder.

The Executioner gave no further attention to the hired gun whose wound stained the green grass beneath him.

After retrieving the M-1 and recharging both it and Big Thunder, Bolan left the open area and faded into the timbered slopes above.

Time to survey the compound.

The intel fed from Stony Man Farm was right on target. A group of armed unknowns had set up shop in Paradise Valley. And an organization capable of fielding hardguys like those whose bodies littered the mountain landscape had to have money and a need for absolute security. None of this was good for America's health.

Bolan eyed the position of the sun, calculated the effect of the high mountains in terms of early nightfall, then blended into the tree-cast shadows. His analysis of the area had to be right the first time. Once the big guy made his final decision, there could be no turning back.

4

KURT HOLBEIN SIPPED the strong black coffee and licked his lips to savor the beverage. He leaned back in his chair and propped his boots comfortably on top of the small desk that filled the center portion of the cubicle he called his office.

Not at all what the tall man desired, but it beat moving from place to place, hiding in attics or damp, darkened basements for days on end. Again he touched the cup to his lips. Leadership had its rewards, and no one deserved such rewards more than Kurt Holbein.

Outside, the clear Colorado mountain air bathed the compound as the sun shone down from a cloudless sky. Inside, the temperature remained constant. Due to the building's careful construction, even the roar of the diesel generator was nothing more than a muted hum in the background.

Kurt Holbein had only one regret, that he had not seen much of the United States, the nation he was pledged to destroy.

He glanced at the heavy gold watch that adorned his right wrist.

Damn the woman. What was taking her so long? If she was not the most brilliant medical specialist in the movement, her lack of speed would not be tolerated. She should have phoned him twenty minutes ago.

He reached for the phone, then withdrew his hand, settling instead for the coffee cup. He would give her another fifteen minutes. Then, if she had not called, Kurt would walk the length of the long corridor and visit the bitch in her laboratory.

Bitch. He thought the single word without anger. Kurt Holbein was past being angry with Lavinia Vitalli. Impatient, yes. Angry, no.

Her work was brilliant, the product of a beautifully warped and twisted mind. That a savage mind such as hers could be harbored in a flawless body did not strike him as out of the ordinary. The minds of all those who rose to the ranks of leadership or specialty in the organization were bent in some manner. It was a group in which deviation was the norm.

As project director, Kurt exercised power even beyond the authority he held over the hundred or so occupants of the compound dubbed Paradise Valley. Although this was just the beginning, Lavinia's work was almost completed. Several of the formulas she developed and tested were ready for wider field testing. He allowed himself a grin of anticipation at the thought.

Drop a vial into the water supply of a small town and sit back to enjoy the results. Formula Hyperactivity 27 (HA-27) was ready for extensive testing now. Tonight, when Kurt could catch the ear of the Great Man, Maurice LeValle, he would propose an immediate testing of HA-27.

What a splendid concept. One part per ten million in a community's water, and all who drank the liquid would become possessed by a restlessness that could not be denied. Rapid movement of hands, arms, feet and legs would occur within minutes after drinking the contaminated water. An irrepressible urge to move would become overpowering. The body would be constantly agitated.

Double the concentration to two parts in ten million and the results were even more extreme. The victim, human or animal, had no choice but to submit to the demands transmitted by the central nervous system. With frenzied activity, running from place to place, the victim would bounce off fixed objects like a possessed billiard ball.

For Holbein, the experimental subjects given HA-27 in the laboratory had afforded him considerable amusement. But it was nothing akin to the pleasure he would get when HA-27 was introduced into the domestic water supply of an American city.

And after tonight's meeting, after LeValle arrived here by helicopter in the dead of night, perhaps Holbein might be able to persuade the Great Man to allow field testing even before the week's end.

Again he sipped the dark brown liquid. Lavinia Vitalli was a genius. Her knowledge of chemicals and his own ability to launch terror strikes would link their names in history. Soon the kingdom of Kurt Holbein would extend far beyond the peaceful mountain valley and would encompass a continent. The thought brought him pleasurable calm.

The phone at his elbow rang.

"Yes."

"I'm ready." The connection was broken the instant Lavinia uttered the two words.

Holbein slowly cradled the receiver. Bitch.

Rising with surprising grace, the project leader walked the length of the white corridor that linked his office with the laboratory where Lavinia Vitalli labored eighteen to twenty hours daily.

Ah, yes, he thought, Lavinia will be successful with her new project too. HA-27's effects will be nothing compared to the drug now being perfected. With the development of her second experimental drug, the power of mind control would be his.

Lavinia's second project would grant power far beyond that ever dreamed of by the world's most grasping dictators, power never even fractionally achieved by the most authoritarian governments the world had known.

Kurt clenched his fists into tight knots.

First, test HA-27 in the field. Then gradually use Lavinia's newest drug to control the minds of the people. His eyes glowed at the thought.

A blank-eyed youth of fifteen or sixteen viewed Kurt without curiosity as the terrorist leader approached. Methodically the boy pushed the broom the length of the already spotless corridor. Yes, Lavinia's drugs worked. She could alter an individual's mind to the point at which he or she was receptive to any and all orders issued. That was the solid first step.

But problems still existed. At first, death resulted within forty-eight hours of the mind-numbing injection. Once that obstacle was overcome, a second presented itself. A totally receptive mind was not capable of any self-direction. The youth sweeping the floor was a case in point. As long as he was told to sweep, and for as long as he lived, the boy swept, but only in the corridor where he was assigned. In order to have a second corridor cleaned, it was necessary to have a guard take him by the hand and move him to a second hall. Otherwise, he would continue indefinitely at the task assigned. But it was still a remarkable step forward. And Lavinia gave him every assurance that a mind subject to being successfully programmed was soon to become reality.

The possibilities played in Kurt's inventive mind. An aerial mist sprayed from a low-flying plane or helicopter under cover of darkness onto agricultural lands.... Cattle would eat the corn, humans would eat the butchered beef. Thousands of people who ate the meat would no longer be their own masters.

Smiling at his thoughts, Holbein entered Lavinia's workplace. As usual, the sight of her aroused him.

Because she wore no bra, her taut nipples were clearly outlined under her smock. Her raven hair was cut short, forming a dark halo that shone brightly around the olive beauty of her face. She had a slender throat and high, full breasts. Her narrow waist flared to full and sensuous hips; she had long slim legs. Her body was as stunning as her mind.

"The pair I injected yesterday died half an hour ago." She did not look up from her writing.

Kurt ground his teeth in silent frustration. And with LeValle coming in less than a dozen hours! At least HA-27 was ready for demonstration.

"What went wrong?" Holbein asked, fighting to keep his voice steady. Long ago he had learned not to shout or try to verbally bully the lovely woman. Once he had done that. Just once. That night Lavinia had taken him to her bed for the third time. She had treated him to a display of her physical abilities that had left him spent and gasping.

Then she refused him for two months. Just as bad, she had refused to allow him to watch the results of the injections she administered. No fool, Kurt understood the message. Never again did he raise his voice to the lovely Lavinia.

"I've made a change. Perhaps it will provide the reaction we desire. Have the retarded boy brought to me in an hour or so."

The retarded boy—like the old man, and the wino who did not know where he was, and the arthritic woman from the nursing home, which had probably failed to report her disappearance for weeks or even months, and like the runaways and hitchhikers—was one of those whom Holbein's men had spirited away from society without their absence being felt.

The tall, blond terrorist rubbed his hands in anticipation. Lavinia, shorter by half a foot, darker by centuries of breeding, noted the gesture and smiled inwardly. Kurt was such a simple man. One day she ought to allow him to sample the delights of HA-27 firsthand. But that little pleasure was in the future. For the present she needed him to deal with the administrative details while she put her mind solely to the task before her.

Holbein spoke. "Herr LeValle will expect a demonstration of HA-27 tonight."

"For that I plan to use the old woman who came in yesterday."

"Splendid."

"Or maybe the girl they call Kathy. She's younger, stronger, better able to demonstrate the full range of hyperactivity to Maurice." Lavinia knew full well Holbein's personal plans for the attractive teenaged girl.

"I think the old woman would be better." His jaw was firm.

"Perhaps. I may need the old one sooner, for a follow-up if the retarded boy fails to respond properly."

He clenched his fists in frustration. The girl was his. Damn the problems. Never did they have enough subjects.

Someone tapped lightly on the door. Lavinia called for identification.

"Raul," said the guy as he entered. The block-headed Raul Hernandez, his eyes dark marbles and his facial features smooth, was head of camp security.

"Patrol group three reported taking two prisoners earlier. When the patrol leader failed to report again at his assigned time a second patrol was sent out. Group six consisted of five members. It has not reported. We must assume both units are lost to us.''

As he delivered his report, his eyes unflinchingly met the gaze of the project leader. Being no fool, the security chief was taking the opportunity of shifting all blame onto the shoulders of the project director.

"Eight men gone?"

"Eight."

"How many of the enemy are in the field?''

Raul shrugged, his attitude suggesting that if he had such information, he would long since have shared it.

"Do not send out more patrols. Were the two units fully capable?''

"My men are always capable," Raul said.

"Of course. That being the case we must assume superior numbers of well-trained attackers. Place your forces on red alert. No one is to leave the compound.''

"I've already done so."

Kurt's breathing and heartbeat were wildly out of balance as he considered the possibilities. They were under siege. The only option open was to defend the compound. How many men opposed them? A dozen, a hundred? To his knowledge, Americans simply did not act in this aggressive fashion.

So who was it out there?

"We'll defend the compound," he said. "When the pilot contacts, have word relayed for him to come in real high and be careful of snipers."

"Try to capture some of them alive," Lavinia said to Raul. "I can always use more subjects."

HE LEFT WITHOUT LOOKING BACK. Had he been in the open, Raul would have spat out his disgust at them. Theirs was a sickness revolting to the security head.

Veteran of eleven successful operations, including the assassination of a United States diplomat in Paris, Raul Hernandez felt soiled by his association with the pair.

Unconscious of his own actions, Raul took a deep breath of the mountain air the minute he left the medical building. He held his lungs full until the feeling of having breathed putrid air had left. Then he exhaled forcefully. He scanned the forested mountain slopes that surrounded the fortified compound like a vast bowl of green.

How many were out there? When would

they attack? Was he in the scope of a sniper who was centering cross hairs on his chest? Raul gave himself a mental shake. He had orders to give and the defense of the compound to supervise. This was no time for fantasy or fear.

Or maybe it was.

5

KEEPING WELL BACK in the trees where his
black form blended with the shadows, Mack
Bolan moved rapidly along the mountain's
flank to a point where the compound below
came into view, locating a jumble of rocks
from which he could study the area without
fear of being observed.

With practiced hands he extracted his
10x50 Bausch & Lombs and began to scan the
area, gathering on-site intelligence before the
sun sank behind the crests of the 13,000- and
14,000-footers.

Bolan could have superimposed his mental
picture of the compound on the actual site
and not been in error in any respect. This was
a tribute to the high quality of the aerial
photographs gathered by USAF jets as much
as it was to the computerlike mind of the warrior. With grim satisfaction he noted various
landmarks that had been fixed in his mind

from his intense study of the recon photos. Everything was just as he envisioned it, from the original ranch structure to the newly built bunkerlike buildings of cement block, to the eight-foot fence that formed the outer perimeter.

Bolan noted that a third patrol unit had not been dispatched from the safety of the enclosure to search for the two that had failed to return. His lips twitched in a brief smile at the knowledge. Circle the wagons!

That suited him fine. Let the hired guns sweat a bit while they awaited the attack they knew would come with the setting of the sun. He would not disappoint them in that respect, though his attack would not come in quite the form they anticipated.

When Raul Hernandez crossed the open space between a building and his awaiting officers, Bolan spotted him at once. He identified Hernandez for what he was—a canny leader whose word was law. After mentally recording the man's description, Bolan turned his attention to the other activities inside the compound.

No one, he noted, approached the heavy wire fence that established the effective limits of the compound itself. A hundred yards of cleared ground lay between the fence and the compound's inner reaches. His rifleman's eye noted the fields of fire offered by the location of the newly erected buildings that formed a rough circle around a large building in the center of the compound.

He accepted that building as his ultimate goal. Within minutes he knew the location of the motor pool, mess facilities, barracks and supply. Though he could not be certain, Bolan assumed the armory was part of the supply building.

He returned his attention to the open area between the buildings and the fence and to the area immediately beyond the fence. With the finely ground binoculars' help, Bolan located an electronic sensor. Next he deduced the pattern in which the others would be placed.

There they were, tiny devices mounted on short steel posts, the sensing unit enclosed in a molded plastic shield to protect it from the elements.

Instinctively Bolan identified the protective field provided by the sensors as the work of the man he'd already pegged as security head. The sensors had been put in place in the same manner as the man moved. Professionally.

It took a bit longer, but Mack Bolan's patience paid off. He spotted one, then two, then a dozen small bare spots in the area between fence and compound. They were the tops of housings for security lights, disguised with a layer of dust.

For seconds more he scanned the area until the location of each light pit was implanted in his memory. Then he gave his attention to the compound itself.

One major change had occurred during the time he studied the area. Every vehicle was now under cover.

Must be getting jumpy down there.

The construction of the new buildings added to the respect Bolan accorded the security chief. Fire sites abounded. Should an intruder manage to get past the fence and survive the next hundred yards of hell, the compound itself offered an invading force no safe cover whatsoever from deadly cross fire.

Bolan turned his attention to a man raking the gravel in front of the motor pool. Bolan studied the worker. While most of the men in fatigues glanced warily toward the encircling mountains from time to time, this man kept his head down and continued to rake without ever looking up. While other men kept close to the walls of the concrete-block structures, this fellow worked in the open.

Bolan made an almost infinitesimal adjustment to the focusing knob. He saw that the man's fatigues were spotless but lacked the razor-sharp creases of those he had encountered already. His fatigue cap was regular issue, not the blocked hat worn by the others, and his boots lacked the high luster Bolan had come to expect.

It was his movements that really set him apart from the others. Like a robot. Automaton. His movements were mechanical, and they never varied. He reached forward the same distance each time with the rake, then drew it toward him at exactly the same speed.

Bolan moved his binoculars in search of another who matched the pattern set by the raker. He found three within a minute. One was painting a building that was already well painted. The second polished an immaculate CJ-5. The third robotlike man stacked cement blocks.

Bolan lowered the glasses and continued along the mountain's brow for another three hundred yards before stopping again to study the compound. From his new vantage point he saw something that had not been apparent before. The outer fence contained a gate.

Worn paths in the valley's sod, visible from where he stood, indicated the gate was much used.

He had seen all he needed to now. He sank back into the shadows of the trees.

The nightscorcher awaited the night. Something grim was happening in Paradise, and Bolan would scourge it thoroughly.

That was the essence of his plan. The precise methods of the plan involved somewhat different criteria than the spiritual obligations that informed the big picture. They were more expedient, and more careful.

Mack Bolan did not want any innocents in the cross fire. Nor did he want to exceed his jurisdiction as the Executioner of the Already Condemned.

He had to infiltrate this place, and neutralize whatever he found there. The evidence of his own eyes insisted on it. But *how* he did it was circumscribed by many factors, from mercy to inaccurate data, that always refined Bolan's ultimate approach.

Just like in Japan on his last mission, just like in the Florida Everglades where Dr. Bruce, the biochemist, had been held, just like in Colombia and the first terrorist compound he encountered in his new war—Bolan was faced with the facts and with a decision.

Something was cooking in this hideout, and a bunch of guys had already tried to kill to guard it; so it was time.

Time to bust in.

AARON KURTZMAN gave his full attention to the screen in front of him. The Bear's expression turned grave as the computer console transmitted information.

April's inquiring look and raised brows spoke her unasked question.

"It's in reply to yesterday's query. NSA tentatively confirm the entry of Kurt Holbein into the States from Canada six months ago. He was traveling under the name of Hans Schmidt, or at least that was on the passport he used when he deplaned at Toronto."

Holbein. The name was familiar in the Stony Man War Room. The guy was an organizer, a director, a European activist greedy for personal power. Though not a field man himself, Holbein had a reputation for choosing those who were capable of carrying out his orders effectively and without question.

"Is there a connection?"

The thick fingers of The Bear danced to a tune of his own composition as they traveled back and forth across the console's keyboard.

"All I can do is ask the proper questions," he said.

It was the waiting that was hardest. While Mack was facing the unknown, April Rose found it all but impossible to remain almost two thousand miles away, trying to be outwardly sane. She had to.

Uncertainty nagged at her thoughts. The recon photo that had arrived after Mack was already in the field, showing the coyotes, and now the response from Washington verifying Kurt Holbein's presence in the country: too many things were coming in just a fraction too late to be useful to Mack Bolan. April was not superstitious, at least not in the normal sense of the word. Yet the timing bothered her. It was as though some warning was being sounded and there was no way she could interpret it or share it with the man who meant everything to her.

6

DUSK CAME EARLY to the mountain valley as the lofty peaks blocked the sun's rays. While on the plains and prairies it was still light, the valley was falling prey to the dark.

Bolan rose from where he rested in a soft carpet of fallen pine needles and tiny boughs. He brushed a few clinging bits from his black skintight suit, which was insulated for warmth.

Silently he moved as a black shadow on the dark mountainside. His evaluation of the compound and its defenses indicated the easiest approach was from the west, where a forested belt came to within fifty yards of the outer fence.

Therefore Bolan planned his initial thrust from the east.

Though this entailed crossing an extra few hundred yards of open mountain meadow, he considered it worth the effort. He knew with grim certainty that the compound's defenders expected him from the west and would put their best marksmen on the western perimeter.

The big warrior did not intend to completely disappoint the defenders on the west, however. When he reached a rock cluster that he had pinpointed earlier, he eased his powerful body into the prone position. He put the M-1 to his shoulder with practiced ease. It was a long time since he had used the weapon, and he had missed it. Memories of earlier wars came to him as the gun nestled in his shoulder. This was the gun and the Smith & Wesson Startron night sight he had used just before Konzaki had joined Stony Man Farm as armorer. Konzaki had known of Bolan's sniper record and was impressed by his continued brilliant handling of the M-1. But he had urged Mack to try other guns and other configurations in the unfolding terrorist wars, and Mack had done so with great success. In the meantime Konzaki had worked on the M-1, played around with it for a bit, and now it was ready for some more action in Bolan's unceasing campaign.

Though near-dark covered the land, the passive infrared scope put the existing light to good use. Just over one hundred yards away, Bolan sighted on one of the sensors he had located earlier in the day.

His forefinger caressed the trigger, and 150 grains of .30-caliber accuracy spiraled from the muzzle of the M-1.

The sensing unit became a haze of particles as the slug put an immediate end to the device. Bolan swung the M-1 forty-five degrees. Again the Startron proved its worth. And again a sophisticated electronic sensor fell prey to the brute force of the 150-grain slug.

Bolan could all but sense the confusion within the base.

The incoming rounds were falling far short of the compound—they were not even reaching the fence.

He took out a third sensor.

An autocarbine chattered its reply. Bolan heard the order that stilled the weapon. Apparently at least one of the troops was shaken to the point of forgetting his training. The thing about fear that was useful to Bolan was that it tends to infect.

Without haste, Bolan left his fire site and moved through the shadowy woods toward his left, toward the north. Three sensors were no longer capable of transmitting. One guard was frightened, the others edgy. Let them sweat. And, hopefully, let them concentrate on the western perimeter with its now-useless sensors.

Ever since the fading rays of the sun gave way to the dark of early evening, Bolan had been aware of the coyote sounds that carried across the moonless meadow. The crafty animals were chuckling and yipping to one another. As the dark deepened, their cries grew in number and volume.

Though people usually associated coyotes with the plains, Bolan knew that the wily animals lived in the mountains to the height of timberline and beyond.

He looked through the Startron at the area of the back gate to the north of the compound. About twenty-five yards from the gate and its well-used path was a depression in the contour of the land. He noted that the light covering of vegetation in this shallow pit was worn down. He could also see little splinters of white. He could not identify what they were.

The worn vegetation suggested that countless animal paws had pressed at the grass. It was too early to be sure about the bits of white. Though Bolan figured he knew the answer, he was willing to wait for an on-site inspection to verify his suspicions.

Suddenly he saw two dozen coyotes approach the depression. The animals must know something. One or two of the beasts lifted slim muzzles and responded to the cries of coyotes still well out in the meadow.

Bolan detected a new sound in the night. It was the muted rattle of chain and lock being opened. He let the Startron pick up the gate. Two men were there. One was quietly slipping the chain free of the gate while the other stood, bent forward slightly.

Why would men expose themselves as targets when they knew something was going down?

Were they insane?

Bolan peered at them through the night scope. In front of the second man was a wheelbarrow, the size used by construction workers. Several bits of cargo hung over the sides of it.

Once the gate was open, the man pushing the barrow moved steadily toward the depression. The other remained at the gate.

Bolan noted the moving man's robotlike

attitude. Looking neither to the right or left, the man advanced steadily, his shoulders hunched slightly with the effort.

Eager coyotes ringed the depression ahead but made no move to advance.

The fellow gained speed slightly as gravity gave a helping hand. Once at the base of the shallow pit the automaton upended the wheelbarrow.

Its cargo tumbled free in a jumble of arms and legs. Human arms and legs.

Without glancing back, the man returned to the building.

Yeah, the perfect solution to the world's labor problems. Turn men into goddamn dog food.

Bolan had come to this remote region at zero notice and with precious little data because it was a job for John Phoenix—the signs were strong that the kind of actions already observed by Stony Man Farm at Bolan hit sites in North Africa and Florida were being imitated in the high reaches of the Rockies. And Bolan, a.k.a. Colonel John Phoenix, had begun the probe immediately, always aware of the time factor of Phoenix's world, where everything is a few short numbers away from exploding and only constant attrition by an ace dealer of death can avert major disaster. This was the Phoenix work zone. He was at home in it. The future of the compound before him was in very serious question.

He moved rapidly.

The coyotes retreated at his coming, tails down, lips curled. The scent of gunmetal overcame their expectation of food. Grudgingly they turned from the feast and waited in panting expectation.

Once in the depression, Bolan slipped a red-lensed light from its slit pocket. The pencil-thin beam of light could not be spotted by even the sharpest-eyed observer at a distance of more than 100 yards.

The scene outlined by the beam of light was exactly what Bolan had anticipated. Still it disgusted him. The bits of white that littered the ground were fragments of bone left by hungry coyotes. Bolan was in the midst of an open-air burial ground, a feeding station for coyotes. Sure, it was the easiest way of disposing of bodies. Take them out and leave them for the animals. It took no great amount of guesswork to deduce where the bodies came from. Experiments involve failures. Failures produced corpses.

With the toe of his boot Bolan stirred at the pressed earth at his feet. More slivers of bone appeared.

The red light caught a semicircle of coyotes eyeing him. Tongues lolled, lips grinned to expose well-developed teeth. Other than an occasional yip of disappointment, the animals made no effort to interfere with his inspection.

Now his light sought the evening feast. The first body Bolan studied was male, probably in his late fifties or even a few years older. Thin, fish-belly white except for hands and face, the man had long needed a shave. His growth of black stubble with its spottings of gray appeared even more unwholesome in death. A wino, Bolan told himself.

His partner was younger, firmly muscled, tanned from the waist up. His eyes, open in death, viewed the beam of light in puzzlement. Doug Fletcher? Bolan memorized the man's facial details in case he encountered Josh and his granddaughter. Knowledge was terrible at times. Lack of knowledge was ten times worse. And Hell was knowledge found too late.

Bolan left the feeding ground for the shelter of the trees. Behind him the coyotes attacked their evening feed with a will. Their cries of greed took on a note of frenzy as powerful jaws chewed into dead flesh.

The sounds of tearing meat and the crunching of small bones followed him into the darker shadows.

Just as he reached the belt of trees, a powerful light shone from a point midway between the fence and the buildings of the compound. That answered one question. The lights were high intensity, not infrared. So much the better. Remotely operated, the lights rose from the earth on small hydraulic pillars.

Mack doused the light with a single shot. Just one more thing for the scum to consider, as they crouched and slunk about, awaiting his attack.

He had struck from the west and now from the north. Since the east offered the worst possible point of attack, that was his next destination.

Setting out at an easy lope, Bolan skirted the open meadow until he was about five hundred yards beyond the fence. Only then did he turn toward the south, his path taking him along a line parallel to the eastern edge of the compound.

Dark forms passed at safe distance as increasing numbers of coyotes came to join their relatives in their grisly feast. Bolan welcomed them, for every animal that passed within the effective range of a sensor sent a signal into the compound. To the men on the control boards, each electronic contact meant doubt and that doubt would grow until it became something huge.

And worried minds made mistakes, and mistakes lowered effectiveness, cost lives.

Bolan headed toward the road that led to the compound from the east.

Once within range of the sensors still doing duty in that direction, he would drop into the two-foot drainage ditch running parallel to the road. The ditch, necessary to keep the road from washing out during the melting of winter snow and the falling of spring and summer rains, provided the preliminary cover he needed.

He would crouch in the ditch until he was within three hundred yards of the fence, then drop to his knees for the next couple of hundred yards. Then he would complete the journey on his belly, and the fence would be his.

Bolan stood stock still. A slight breeze, downslope now that night was upon the mountains, carried with it the sound of a laboring engine. The vehicle was too far from the open meadow to be seen, its lights still lost in the road's twisting and turning. It was quickly approaching.

Bolan resumed his ground-covering lope. The plan had to be changed.

7

THE BIG GUY was lying prone a dozen yards
from the road when the van emerged from the
line of trees bordering the high mountain
valley. Careful not to diminish his night vision by looking into its lights, Bolan studied
the oncoming van.

It was not possible to tell what the vehicle
contained in the way of men or weapons or
how many occupied the cab area.

Take it out or let it pass? The decision was
his to make.

Putting aside the M-1, Bolan drew from its
elongated holster the silenced Beretta 93-R
autopistol.

When the van was twenty yards away,
Bolan closed one eye and aimed toward it.
The autopistol chugged once and a 9mm slug
cored through the near rear tire of the van. A
second silenced cough and a front tire burst
from the gun's crushing power.

Both eyes open now, his night vision still perfect—the result of having kept one pupil in the dark while looking at the van's lights— the shadow in black moved with all the speed his powerful legs could provide.

The driver was still fighting the wheel. He was a hard-eyed individual whose qualifications would inevitably include political assassination and mutilation with car bombs. He was clawing for his .357 as Bolan wrenched open the passenger door of the still-moving vehicle. There was no contest.

The Beretta uttered its cough as Bolan ran alongside the open door, the 9mm parabellum slug ending the driver's efforts to draw his own weapon. The van came to a juddering halt, its headlights blazing into the deep dark of the mountain evening.

Bolan reached across to twist the ignition key but left the lights glowing. The driver slumped forward, his forehead resting on the top edge of the steering wheel as blood pulsed onto the dash.

Mack Bolan was again in motion. In half a dozen long-legged strides he was at the rear door of the commercial-sized rig.

With the Beretta at the ready, he tried the rear doors. The handle turned without resisting. He snapped the metal door open and twisted his body into attack position.

Inside the back of the van an overhead light gleamed in a feeble effort to push back the night. Two men crouched motionless near the front of the cargo space. Both peered out the open door with wide, questioning eyes. One man was young, probably in his early twenties. The other was middle-aged, his frail body and telltale smell identifying him as another wino.

Bolan eased his muscular body into the back of the van. He allowed the door to swing shut, but not latched behind him.

"What are you doing here?" he asked the younger of the pair.

"I was hitching. Next thing I knew a guy was pointing a cannon at me. They slapped cuffs on me and tossed me in with this poor bastard."

Bolan slid the Beretta into its snag-free holster and slipped the carbon-steel cutters from his belt. He extended the red-lensed light toward the younger man.

"Hold this on his cuffs."

The wino offered no protest as Bolan cut the cuffs from his thin wrists. Then Bolan turned his attention to the younger, stronger captive. The kid flinched, yelped in surprise as the tips of the cutter caught the flesh of one wrist.

"Hold still." Bolan's tone of voice stopped any further protest.

Once he had the pair free, Bolan pointed to the rear of the van.

"Follow the road back. It will lead to a larger road eventually."

The big guy reopened the van's rear doors and swung lightly to the ground, careful to look into the night's dark as he did so.

Cramped, numb, the two captives slowly followed Bolan's lead.

The sound of a second vehicle approaching from the east came clearly to the night fighter. The pair seemed unaware of its nearness.

"Get off the road, drop flat!" Bolan ordered.

The two hesitated and he propelled them headlong with a solid push. Stumbling, the two plunged into the open meadow. Bolan followed their bumbling progress with ears only. They were in no danger now if they used their heads. He had given them help. Whether they rose or fell was up to them.

At Bolan's side the van's twin taillights

shone ruby red onto the narrow path of raw earth.

Bolan faded into the darkness to prepare for the oncoming vehicle. As he brought the Beretta to full firepower, he considered retrieving the M-1 but rejected the idea. He would stick to the silenced weapon and continue his quiet war.

It was a Jeep, probably another CJ-5. Bolan identified it from its engine's sound as it roared out of the forest belt. Lights on full bright, it rocketed forward, the driver unaware that the red glow of lights ahead came from a halted van.

When he realized the first vehicle was motionless, the driver braked hard, then was forced to whip the steering wheel back and forth as he corrected and overcorrected for the Jeep's bouncing skid. He brought his bucking vehicle to a halt only twenty yards behind the stricken van.

The Executioner was already in motion when the Jeep stopped. Bolan snapped a silent slug through the driver-side windshield.

His action drew an instant response from one of the passengers, though Bolan's flash hider prevented his position being revealed. A withering hail of .22 sizzlers spewed from the snout of a 180 autocarbine.

Rolling as he hit the ground, Bolan snapped another jacketed missile through the Jeep's front glass. A grunt of pain mingled with surprise rewarded him.

The man's answering fire was high and wide. Aiming at the series of muzzle-flashes, Bolan fired in three-shot bursts. Behind the windshield, the guard lowered his autocarbine for the final time. Sightlessly he stared down at two entry holes that joined the first, ruining the press of his fatigue shirt. The back of the seat was savaged by exiting slugs that ripped flesh, bone and tissue from the dying body and plastered it to the fabric covering the Jeep's passenger seat.

The third member of the crew had opened fire over his dead companions. Rather than return the fire, Bolan rolled half a dozen times to his left, the move taking him well clear of the tight-clustered bursts from the 180.

The hardguy was firing blind. He fired in short bursts, spreading in a pattern around the area that Bolan had previously occupied. The guy was playing it by the book.

Bolan's reply was aimed just above the

light flashes and slightly to their left. Half a dozen .22 hummers rose skyward as the man's body was flung back by the force of the 9mm slug that shattered one rib, glanced off a second, then tore away his lung.

On single-shot the Beretta sighed yet another silent cough and the guard's heart exploded, blood spurting from its savaged upper chamber.

Bolan gave the vehicle and its crimsoned contents no further attention. It was time to breach the compound fence.

He left the van and CJ with lights still aglow behind him. The vehicles' beams shone as though to ward off attack from the dark meadow.

Yeah, Bolan thought as he gathered his M-1, let them wonder, and worry and wait. The more attention centered on the pair of motionless vehicles, the better his chances of slipping through the fence elsewhere, and across a hundred yards of no-man's land.

Mack Bolan became a shadow in a composition of black on black.

RAUL HERNANDEZ stood three paces behind a pair of men manning the electronic control panels.

"Well?" The single word expressed his impatience with the two men, with the lack of hard intelligence available to him and with the entire operation.

"I think I'm just picking up animal movement, sir."

"You think? You don't know?" Even as he spoke, Raul knew he was allowing his own uncertainty to surface.

"Keep at it," the commander said.

The door to the control room opened and closed without Hernandez turning. Gino Cabelli, his third-in-command, came to his side.

One of two persons privileged to address Hernandez by his given name, Gino began his report. His voice betrayed no trace of emotion.

"We're surrounded, Raul. At least on three sides."

"What about the van? Has it moved?"

"No. Its position is unchanged."

"And the patrol unit?"

"Their final transmission said they had the van in view. There was no follow-up."

Raul turned away from him. "Better they had remained guarding the main entrance."

Gino kept his own counsel. It had been his suggestion that the outlying unit be brought up at the last minute to provide cover for the nearly defenseless van.

"How many out there?" Raul turned to glare at him.

Gino referred to his clipboard. "Two, perhaps three confirmed from the west. All sharpshooters. Another two to the north. To the east—" he raised his tailored shoulders in a slight shrug "—at least half a dozen. That unit was among our best."

"Any identifiable gunshots other than our 180s?"

"Perhaps one or two autocarbines. Those on the east side were uncertain."

"No other weapons?" Raul's voice was harsh.

"Not that our men heard."

"Move three men from each of the west, north and east walls. Put them on the south."

"Sir." The response held an unvoiced question.

"That is the direction from which the main thrust will come."

Gino turned on his polished heel to do his chief's bidding. Not once in the seven missions in which he had served with Raul had the leader made a serious error.

"Gino." It brought the third-in-command

to an instant halt. "What of the north gate?"

"It . . . it's still open."

"Have it closed."

"But it isn't electronic. . . ."

"Have it closed."

Gino Cabelli left the command room.

Raul studied the jumble of cybernetic devices over the heads of the two men. A dozen enemy on three sides. There would be much distracting fire when the attack became a reality. How many would come from the south? How would they breach the outer fence? Grenades, maybe. Satchel charges or plastique more likely.

He approached the two technicians. "Have the perimeter lights turned on and off in ones and twos, but follow no set pattern," he said. "Order the men to fire at anything near the fence."

"Yes, sir." Low-voiced commands began at once while fingers danced to shut off the lights.

He knew it would not stop the attack but it might diminish its effectiveness.

Another thought came to him. Perhaps the attack would be all-out, lacking the diversionary fire he anticipated. That would add another dozen to the attacking force. Which would bring the total to twenty-five? Fifty? How many died when the 180s chattered in the dark? How many of the attacking force were no longer able to advance against the compound?

Mentally Raul added his own losses. Eight earlier in the day. One more at the north gate—the coyote gate, as many knew it. Now three possibly lost on the road. And two more in the van. More than a dozen good men gone, and nothing to show for it.

Raul Hernandez set his mind to work on the problem.

It had to be simple, yet devastatingly effective.

For minutes he stood unmoving. Then his thin lips changed expression, becoming a cruel smile.

8

THE OVERHEAD LIGHT SHONE with a glow that gave the white interior of the small room the appearance of hospitallike sterility. Except for a stool, the room's only furniture consisted of a pair of narrow cots pressed against opposite walls.

She sat on the cot farthest from the room's locked door. Her slim legs, bare except for cut-off jean shorts and ragged sneakers, were pulled up toward her chin. The girl's worn T-shirt bore the slogan "Another Fine California Pair" and featured the picture of two large pears, each atop one of her breasts.

Her flawless skin was shining from her recent scrubbing in the tiny basin of water that she was given daily. Her brown eyes regarded her new cellmate with compassion.

"I'm Kathy O'Connor," she said. "Did you just arrive?"

"I'm Elsa Moore and I arrived yesterday.

Before that I resided at the Kellington Home for the Aged in Denver.'' The elderly woman's voice was firm, a contrast to her obviously frail body.

"I'm glad to have some company," Kathy admitted, quickly adding, "but not happy they brought you here."

"And just exactly where is here?"

"We're somewhere in the mountains. They got me in Denver, too. The van was enclosed, so I didn't see a thing. But I listened to traffic sounds and later to the driver gearing down, and I'm sure we're in the mountains maybe fifty miles or so from Denver."

Elsa Moore agreed. She had already undergone some dawning of the truth of her mysterious transfer. For the better part of an hour the two talked quietly.

Kathy twice left her cot's minimal comfort to pour water from her carefully rationed supply so that the elderly woman could moisten her dry lips and parched throat. Several times their conversation stopped in mid-sentence as the sound of booted feet came to them through the space beneath the door. Each time the footsteps either halted before reaching their holding room or went past. And each time Kathy exhaled the breath she held, unaware that she did so.

"And who are these people, these kidnappers?" Elsa asked at last.

"They wear some sort of army uniforms. At least the guards do. The man in charge is called Kurt Holbein." Kathy's lips pulled into a grimace as she spoke the name. "Raul Hernandez is in charge of the guards." She hesitated, then remained silent.

The old woman peered at the attractive young girl and waited, her bright eyes missing nothing. Finally Elsa Moore broke the silence.

"Tell me about the one you really fear, Kathy."

The girl's head came up, taking her chin from her knees. She regarded the old woman with frank curiosity.

"What are you, Mrs. Moore, some kind of mind reader?"

The old woman's chuckle gave no evidence of concern for self or future. "Kathy, I'm eighty-two years old. If a person hasn't learned something about human nature in that time, then she hasn't paid much attention to what was going on around her all those years."

After glancing at the door as though the dreaded person might materialize there, Kathy said, "Her name is Lavinia. I don't know her last name. She always wears some sort of white coat like a doctor. She just makes my skin crawl. It's something about her."

"A feeling of evil?"

"That's it exactly. She's evil. She reminds me of a really beautiful jungle animal, but when I look into her eyes I have the feeling she'd like to claw me to bits."

Again the elderly woman nodded her understanding. Slowly, carefully, she re-arranged her birdlike limbs on the edge of the the narrow cot. "My joints get stiff when I stay too long in one position," she explained. "You mentioned listening to traffic and hearing the driver change gears. That means you were conscious during your ride."

Kathy hesitated, then nodded her head. "I was awake."

"Where in Denver did they capture you? I assume you did not come of your own free will."

"I was walking along the street. It was pretty late at night. A couple of guys in this van pulled up to the curb and I went over to them. They grabbed me, and before I really knew what was happening I was handcuffed to a ring in the back of the van.''

"You didn't call out for help?"

"The guy riding with me, one of the two guys who grabbed me, he'd have knocked my head off."

"He rode in back with you?"

"Yeah, he sure did."

Aware of the careful scrutiny of the older woman, Kathy hugged her knees closer to her body.

"And he abused you during your journey." It was a statement, not a question.

"If you mean he raped me on the floor of the van, I guess he abused me."

"And since you arrived?"

Kathy snorted, then grinned a mocking smile intended only for herself. "It hasn't been all that bad. Not much worse than the last couple of years, really."

"You're a runaway."

Impulsively, the girl left her cot and moved to sit beside the old woman.

With hesitant tenderness she wrapped her slim arm around the other's frail shoulders. For minutes the two captives sat taking silent comfort from each other.

When Kathy O'Connor began to speak her voice was low, yet strong. She spoke of running away from home two years earlier, of the fears she had had once on her own, and of her determination never to return to her drunken father and her mother.

She spoke of washing dishes in hostels, of sleeping in an alley, of running from gangs of roving juveniles. Eventually she walked the length of East Colfax waiting for someone to offer her the cost of a meal and rent in exchange for her body.

"And how long have you been here?"

"A week. Actually eight days. It hasn't been all that bad. The Nazi, that's what I call Kurt, he likes me. Likes my body. He's not much in bed but at least he's quick. I've been with him four or five times. Raul has only been with me once."

"And Lavinia. Is she jealous? Is that why she seems to be evil to you?"

Kathy shook her head.

"She isn't jealous, at least not of me. She can have any man she wants and she knows it. Kurt is wild for her—I could see it in his eyes when they were together. She's like a black widow."

"You're something of a psychic yourself," Elsa said.

"I've spent my life with creeps and bums, so I understand them."

"Tell me then. What's happening here? Why are we here?"

For seconds it seemed Kathy might not answer. When she began to speak her voice was low, her words muted.

"Some sort of experiment. I don't know for sure. All I know is that whatever happens in here can kill you. That's why they keep bringing in people like you and me. To replace the ones who die."

Instantly Kathy regretted sharing her knowledge. She wished to recall her words, and her face mirrored her dismay.

"Not to worry, Kathy." The bony hand lightly touched the girl's bare knee, then withdrew. "At my age death is merely a matter of the proper time and place. It holds no fear."

For the first time in days, tears blurred Kathy's eyes.

The two women sat in silence, each lost in consideration of what was, what was to be, what might have been. Both Kathy's hands now rested atop her bare legs, her long fingers tightly interwoven to prevent her hands from trembling.

The old woman's right arm was extended behind her to give support to her tired spine while her left hand toyed with her dress, stained from its contact with the bed in the van.

"How soon will they be coming for me?" Elsa Moore's voice held no distress. She simply wanted to know.

Kathy hesitated, considered lying, then dismissed the thought. Her cell mate was the first warm and caring human being she had met in months.

"It all depends. One woman was here when I came. They took her about an hour later. The second woman was with me most of one day. She didn't come back either. And now you're here."

"How many people would you estimate have vanished while you've been here?"

"As nearly as I can tell, seventeen." Her response was automatic. It was a figure she kept current. "No, it may be eighteen. Just before you came I heard them taking the retarded boy out of his room across the hall. I didn't hear them bring him back."

"Retarded?"

"I watched him for a long time yesterday. He just looked retarded. You know, sort of drooled on himself, seemed real clumsy."

Again the pair sat in silence.

The sounds of two pairs of boots advancing along the corridor came clearly.

Kathy listened intently, judging the distance from the door to the stomping feet.

When the steps stopped before the door, the girl let her slim arm encircle the shoulders of the frail little woman.

The knob twisted a quarter turn. Two figures in spotless fatigues entered the room.

Anxiously, Kathy scanned the faces of the pair. Both were alert, wary. Hope died within her. She knew the routine. A guard and a zombie or two zombies meant food. Two guards, no zombies, meant only one thing.

This time, Kathy poised to defend the old woman at her side.

9

USING THE MOONLESS NIGHT to his advantage, Bolan, on his belly, covered the final hundred yards separating him from the fence. With the M-1 cradled in the crook of each elbow, he followed the graded drainage ditch. Though sharp chunks of stone and exposed edges of larger rock bit into his body, Bolan never slowed.

As he covered the final distance to the fence, he saw the glow of high-intensity lights that came and went in the area between the fence and the compound. He lay in the scant shelter offered by the ditch and mentally timed the lights as each glowed for a short time, then joined the night's black. In minutes the warrior was satisfied. The concealed lights were rising above ground and shining for a short time in no specific pattern. Even the duration of their glow varied. A guy who ran the erratic lighting pattern was up against a computer.

Again he advanced, this time until the base of the fence's heavy wire was within easy reach. From one of his slit pockets Bolan withdrew an electronic device no larger than a pack of cigarettes. Two wires that ended in alligator clips dangled free.

Silently saluting the electronic genius of Gadgets Schwarz, Bolan fitted the pair of tiny insulated clips to the fence and made certain each was making solid contact. With his thumbnail he flicked the switch to activate the device. For seconds the little digital dial remained inactive, then the tiny numerals glowed red. Four digits. Eleven hundred volts! The fence was a mankiller.

After three seconds, the lighted indicator lost its color as the four numerals vanished. Twenty-five seconds passed before the numerals reappeared. Again they vanished after three seconds.

Bolan used the next twenty-five seconds to study the main gate just to his left. Because it was electronically operated, Bolan could see no way of opening it from the outside. Not without blasting the hell out of it. Again the tiny numerals glowed red. Twenty-five seconds. Right on schedule.

What about the smaller gate left open on

the northern side of the fence? Did they kill the power for the entire fence when that gate had to be opened? More likely, it was protected by insulators so it could be opened and closed manually. That was a chink in the compound's armor. If there was one such flaw, perhaps there were others.

Twenty-five more seconds elapsed. Again the numerals glowed. Bolan reached for his steel cutters. Even with their insulated handles he did not want to deal with eleven hundred volts; he would wait for the gap.

Call it intuition. Just as he prepared to extend the carbon-steel cutters toward the fence, he hesitated. In that instant the tiny numerals again came to life, even though only eight seconds had passed since the previous charge.

They stayed on for twenty seconds. Then the digital indicator darkened once more. Sixteen seconds later it lit up for twelve seconds, then twenty seconds passed, and again it glowed, this time for eight seconds.

Thus the big guy noted a second chink in the compound's defenses. Despite the staggered charges of the killer current, it was set for total intervals of twenty-eight seconds. He watched it through another pair of cycles to confirm his findings. When the indicator again darkened, Bolan set to work on the fence. The tempered jaws of the cutters nipped through the heavy wire with only the slightest urging as Bolan's wrists transmitted the power of his arms into the instrument.

Allowing himself a safety margin of three seconds in each cycle, it took less than two minutes to open an entry space in the heavy wire, big enough to crawl through but not so complete a gap that it would break the circuit. Replacing the cutters that had served him well in recent hours, Mack folded open the wire during the next cycle.

Ignoring the random glow of the high-intensity lights, Bolan slipped through the hole in the fence. Behind him was the safety of the ditch, plus the firepower of the M-1. Ahead was a fortified compound defended by many dozens of highly trained men.

He spent precious numbers studying the digital readout. Certain he had the current's staggered cycles correct, he prepared to close the gap in the wire. Using the insulated cutters, he pushed the flap of wire back into place. As he worked he heard the chopper blades.

Though Bolan's entry area would be visible

on close inspection, it could not be spotted from a hundred yards. Unless the fence had an electronic break-and-ground detector, his entry would not be known until he decided it should be, and that was the chance he took.

The chopper came in from the southeast. Once the bird reached the open meadow, the pilot changed course and veered sharply from his flight path. With the distinct whump-whump of the main rotor as his guide, Bolan tracked the chopper's movements by ear.

The pilot flew a quick half circle around the open meadow, keeping just above the trees that fringed the mountainsides around the open valley. When the pilot completed 180 degrees, he gained altitude, crossed the open space in a rush and headed for the center of the compound. There it landed.

The chopper's approach indicated the pilot was only too aware the area was under siege. Bolan permitted himself the satisfaction of knowing he had the defenders spooked.

As the main rotor slowed to an idle, Bolan began his crawl across the open area toward his goal. The copter could not have arrived at a better time. It was a distraction. Furthermore, the random glowing of the lights became more his advantage than the guards'.

As each light glowed briefly, the eyes of the men on post automatically turned in that direction in an effort to detect movement. Not only did that destroy any night vision they had, but it kept even the best of men from maintaining total surveillance.

Like a mountain cat with its belly to the ground as it moved toward its prey, Bolan covered the open area, totally committed to his goal, hungry but not greedy, at a peak of alertness.

The compound's lighted center cast a soft glow into the night sky while creating shadows along the edge of the cement-block building that was Bolan's immediate goal. Once he reached the base of the newly constructed building, he crouched to survey the situation.

He heard voices. Words, occasional phrases, but nothing that could identity the group within. Someone important had arrived in the chopper. Bolan listened intently. Whoever had arrived was ahead of schedule. That was fine with Bolan. The more the merrier.

He became aware of movement north of where he crouched. The rising glow of one of the lights revealed a guard bearing his autocarbine as he dropped to one knee, covering his partner, who moved toward the open north gate.

The silenced Beretta 93-R appeared in Bolan's hand, eager to do his bidding. He stealthily moved to within thirty yards of the guy providing cover.

Without pressing closer, Bolan raised the autopistol. At the stroking of his finger the weapon dispatched a 9mm whisper of death into the night—and into the body of the man holding the autocarbine. The jacketed slug found its target just beneath the guard's right armpit. He was flung hard to the side by the bullet's force.

Bolan, his pistol on single-shot, sent a second round. The remaining scout was running for the sanctuary of the compound. The jacketed slug, issued with a slight cough that only the nightscorcher could hear, hit its moving target in the top left of the guy's dark green fatigue shirt. He slumped to the ground as the explosion of his heart brought his forward momentum to an abrupt end.

Mack Bolan turned to look back at the roof line of the building he had just left. He studied it very, very closely.

"I'VE GOT GRIMALDI ON THE LAND LINE." The Bear's voice interrupted the activities of the others who shared the War Room at Stony Man Farm.

The Bear switched over to the wall speaker. The pilot's voice filled the room.

"Nothing to report here, Hal. Striker has been out of radio contact since I left the drop site."

"Most likely Striker's transceiver can't reach you because of the surrounding mountain ridges and peaks," Hal Brognola said into a console microphone.

"Right," Grimaldi agreed.

"Then Mack is on his own again," April Rose said softly, staring directly at her desktop mike.

"Right to a degree, April. I'm more than a hundred miles from his site. Conditions need to be ideal for us to have transmission."

April Rose gazed at the far wall as though she could see through it, as though she could cover the distance that separated her from Mack Bolan.

10

MAURICE LEVALLE MOVED BRISKLY across the raked gravel to get clear of the helicopter. With his left hand holding his graying hair in place and his right holding a thin attaché case, the tall lean man did not glance back.

Ahead of him, Kurt Holbein was leaving the medical building. The project director's thin lips were tightly compressed. He openly looked at his heavy gold watch to let his superior know the irritation he felt at the other's early arrival.

LeValle smiled, transferred the case to his left hand and accepted Holbein's outstretched palm.

"Good to see you, Kurt. And, yes, I am aware I'm ahead of schedule. I only hope my early arrival did not inconvenience you or the lovely Ms. Vitalli."

"Not in the least, Maurice. Your arrival is always an occasion of great pleasure for us.

Coffee? A drink? Perhaps a few minutes to freshen up?''

LeValle's dark eyes locked onto Holbein's.

"Women freshen up, Kurt. Thank you, but no. Let's join Lavinia in her laboratory at once. She is there, is she not?''

"She's there.''

LeValle led the way from the graveled area into the building's interior and to Lavinia's quarters, which he entered without knocking.

"Ah, Lavinia.'' He approached her with both arms held wide, the slender case suspended from his left hand.

Their embrace lasted seconds and held no real warmth. It did, however, cause Kurt's blood to boil.

Without being asked, LeValle selected a chair from one of several surrounding a circular table. Lavinia and Kurt seated themselves on either side of LeValle so that they faced each other across the table.

"Bring me up to date.'' LeValle's tone was chill.

During the next three minutes LeValle sat motionless, only his eyes giving evidence of the attention he gave to the words of Lavinia Vitalli. When her recital ended, the three sat without speaking.

Holbein showed intense interest in studying his long-fingered hands. Lavinia gazed intently at the man in the expertly tailored three-piece suit, while LeValle's eyes focused on a point just beyond the white wall opposite him.

"Too slow. You're not moving rapidly enough," LeValle said finally.

"I have to disagree." Lavinia kept her voice deliberately flat. "We've made enormous progress in the short time allotted to me. I'm at the point of total success. Already we have half a dozen—no, seven—subjects who work daily around the area."

"How many failures?"

Lavinia shrugged to indicate how unimportant her losses were. "What is a failure? I've lost a number of subjects while bringing the drug to perfection. Those were not failures. Laboratory losses are to be expected—they are a necessary part of any scientific procedure."

"Ah, Lavinia. Let us not debate the problem. You were supposed to be beyond that point when you left Italy. And that was nearly six months ago."

"Due to the lack of human subjects, I could do only so much," Lavinia insisted.

"Dogs, monkeys, sheep. I can advance only so far with them. The hyperactivity compound HA-27 is perfect. It requires no further laboratory testing. In fact—" deliberately Lavinia avoided the eyes of Kurt Holbein "—it is ready for field testing. I'd like to suggest we select a test site while you are here this evening and let Kurt get on with it."

Holbein's hands clenched. Feeling Le-Valle's mocking gaze, the project director forced himself to appear relaxed.

"I've already selected several potential test sites for you to consider," Holbein said to LeValle. He would deal with the vicious bitch later, at a time of his choosing.

"Let's return to the problem of mind domination for the moment." LeValle's words were smooth. "I'd like to see a few of your successes."

Lavinia moved to a phone and punched four buttons. She issued an order, recradling the instrument without awaiting a response.

Seconds later a gentle knocking sounded on the laboratory door.

"Come in." Lavinia's voice was just loud enough to carry through the door.

Three middle-aged men, clad in fatigues that showed some lack of care, entered the room. Their movements were mechanical. The door closed firmly behind the three.

Lavinia advanced to meet the trio midway across the room.

"Stop."

The three halted.

"You." She touched one with the tip of her index finger. "Come with me."

He followed as the strikingly beautiful terrorist walked toward the counter that lined most of one wall.

"Use that cloth. Clean the counter." Without waiting to see that he obeyed, Lavinia turned away. The man immediately began to do her bidding.

Lavinia set the second of the trio to work at polishing the already spotless floor of the big room.

The third she ordered to run on the spot.

"Very impressive," LeValle conceded. "I congratulate you. How long will they continue their tasks?"

"Until they are told to do otherwise. Or until they drop from exhaustion." Satisfaction was evident in her tone.

"They cannot be programmed to move from one task to another without supervision?"

"Not yet."

"How soon can you guarantee me a success rate of fifty percent?"

"Soon. Very soon."

"Give me a date."

Holbein's lips softened in a suggestion of a smile as Lavinia worried.

"One month, provided I have a sufficient number of subjects to work with."

LeValle nodded. "One month." Then to Holbein he said, "You will see that Lavinia has an adequate number of subjects with which to work."

It was Lavinia's turn to enjoy the squirming.

"Now," LeValle said as he brought his hands together on the table before him, "let's see your HA-27 in action."

"I think you will be pleased." Lavinia reached for the telephone but hesitated. "Shall I let them continue or have you seen enough?" She gestured in the direction of the three engaged in their routines.

"Quite enough, thank you."

"Kurt, would you see to them while I make this call?" Her voice was silken, honey sweet, her eyes bright with the sense of power.

Had LeValle not been present Holbein

would have risked a verbal confrontation with the woman. As it was, he added yet another mark beside Lavinia's name, each mark indicating one more item that would be repaid.

"It's a female," Lavinia said to LeValle. "Kurt has been slow in obtaining subjects, so we have only two remaining. One is old, the other a girl of about seventeen. I think the girl will provide a better demonstration for us." She punched the first digit on the telephone dial.

"No." Kurt faced the two of them. "You will be needing the girl later for your mind domination work. Best to use the old woman, since this demonstration will result in death."

Lavinia's laughter was mocking. To LeValle she said, "Kurt has been keeping the girl for himself. She's really quite attractive in a thin sort of way."

LeValle's expression was one of interest.

"Is she good?" He directed his question to Kurt.

The project director weighed his responses, finally chosing the proper one.

"She is an interesting diversion after a hard day's work."

"That being the case," LeValle turned to

Lavinia, "let's sacrifice the old one." To Kurt he added, "I will test your assertion later this evening." His smile was sinister in its blandness.

RAUL HERNANDEZ STOOD REGARDING the chopper. He glanced at his watch for the third time in less than three minutes. As long as the machine remained on the ground it was his responsibility. Once it was in the air he could dismiss it from his mind.

His dark, restless eyes surveyed the inner compound. Good men. His troops were alert and on post.

"Sir."

Raul turned. A guard had halted three feet from him.

"Sir, both members of the detail sent to secure the coyote gate have gone down."

"Gone down?"

"Yes, sir. Logan has them in his night glasses. Neither is moving."

"Then the enemy is inside the fence?"

"There is no evidence the fence has been breached."

No evidence? Two men down. Hernandez kept calm against raging uncertainty.

"Thank you. Return to your post. Keep alert."

The chopper rotors began to whirl more rapidly. Thanks to God for small favors. At least the bird was on its way. That still left LeValle under his care, but that was the least of Raul's worries.

Once the helicopter cleared the compound area, Hernandez made a tour of the inner portion of the compound. He found his troops ready and willing to engage the enemy. Not once did Hernandez have reason to find fault.

As he neared the supply building, he withdrew a ring filled to capacity with keys. He approached the darkened building and entered. Snapping on lights as he went, the soldier approached the building's one locked door.

Once in front of the inner door, he used two keys to release the twin locks. Pushing the door open, he stepped into a small but well-equipped armory. He moved to a particular shelf.

Raul gathered five claymore antipersonnel mines from the two dozen available. With them and the necessary detonating devices in hand, he left the small room.

Once at the door, he moved an ammunition carton with his boot to prop the door open. He wanted his troops to have immediate access to this secret source of secondary arms and ammunition. The battle was due.

11

BOLAN STOOD BENEATH THE EAVES of the low building. He reached up with both hands to determine the height. No more than seven feet from the ground to the low point of the eaves. He ran his hands along the composition roofing and felt the tiny grains of rough grit against his fingertips.

He bent slightly at the knees, then with every ounce of power in his legs, he sprang upward. For an instant Bolan feared his spring was not enough to let him straighten his arms on the roof and bring the rest of him up. The rough roofing grit bit into the palms of his hands. He hovered on the brink of failure. Shoulder muscles straining, he leaned forward into the roof to force his body upward. Then he turned his palms a full 180 degrees and raised his body onto the roof.

As he flattened out, the chopper rose from within the compound. Once clear of the buildings the pilot slipped the machine westward through the night's cool, following much the same security approach he had used in landing.

Bolan slithered across the roof. He took his first close look at the compound he intended to storm. He continued to mentally compare it with the aerial photos studied back at Stony Man Farm. His practiced eye took in the positions occupied by the defenders.

What were the odds? Forty, fifty, a hundred to one? A vitally important factor was in Bolan's favor: the site's defenses were always directed toward the perimeter. But Bolan was already deep inside.

Knowing what he must do, he inched his way back the width of half the roof.

He jumped to the ground. The stiletto with its twin razor edges was in his big hand as he long-legged it around the corner of the building.

He came up behind a pair of troops he had seen from the roof.

Bolan's left hand closed over the mouth of the near guard while the stiletto slashed across his exposed throat. A nearly severed head lolled back as eyes gone suddenly sightless peered upward.

The second guard spun to face the night-fighter. Even as he did so, two inches of meticulously honed blade ripped through his larynx, slicing his vocal cords before they could react to the command frantically issued by the brain. The dying nonentity eyed the very special being that was his executioner and in the last split second of his life he was afraid beyond all imagination.

Like one of the night's many shadows, Bolan moved on to the side door of the motor-pool building. Inside, he edged his way around the vehicles. With a wire garrote held between both hands, he crept toward the guards at the front door.

It took a dozen measured heartbeats to reach the nearer of the two guards, who stood looking out into the night a few feet behind the other guard's back. The silent shadow extended its big arms to slip the piano wire over the guy's head, then tightened its muscles to make the cut quick and deep. The thin, all but unbreakable wire sliced into the soldier's throat. Any cry of alarm was cut off before it began.

Bolan eased the sagging body to the ground.

Again his big arms moved. For the second

time in seconds, Bolan struck unawares and cut the odds by one.

The man on point was stronger, more alert than his dead companion had been. With hands made doubly powerful by the realization of his danger, he clawed at the savage wire that had already disappeared into the flesh of his fingertips and throat. His weapon fell as the hardguy gasped for life.

His body tensed in one final contortion. Bolan held it upright by the garrote. Then the big warrior lowered the body to the ground and extracted his killer wire.

Bolan wiped the wire clean on the sleeve of the once immaculately maintained fatigues at his feet.

Within seconds Mack Bolan was again at the heart of the deserted motor-pool building. From a slit pocket, Bolan extracted a piece of plastique.

He worked the waxed-paper covering free and deftly inserted the detonator.

He stashed the hot pack beside the gas tank of one of the Jeeps parked near the center of the wide building. Also stored in this part of the building were 250-gallon drums, painted black and piled on top of each other to keep them as far as possible from the walls. It was the same principle that was functioning to Bolan's advantage in the camp as a whole. The assumption was that the perimeters were where the attack action would be, and that was where the defense agitation should respond.

Whenever Bolan activated the electronic device he carried with him, the entire motor pool and the vehicles that the building sheltered would be eliminated in a sheet of liquid fire.

Bolan moved on.

The lab building had the same small high windows as the mess area. Lights glowed in several of them. Keeping to the shadows, the black-clad invader pushed on into the darker area to the north of the building.

12

WITHOUT GIVING THOUGHT to her impulsive action, Kathy O'Connor faced the pair of guards with clenched fists.

"Leave us alone, you bastards. We're not going anywhere with you."

The taller of the pair, a man whose spotless uniform belied the image created by his grossly ugly face and wandering left eye, snarled a reply.

"All we want is the old bag of bones."

"No!" The single word screamed from Kathy's throat.

The two men crowded into the small room. While the one with the ravaged face reached toward Kathy, his partner stepped to his right in a quick flanking move. The result was predictable.

Even as Kathy's fists unclenched to become raking claws, the battle was lost. A fist caught her on the side of the head. Lights flashed as pain raced to her brain. A round-house hit from Wall-eye that struck open-handed at the opposite side of her face snapped her head back.

Without bothering further with the collapsing girl, the men extended angry hands toward the old woman.

"I can stand by myself." The quiet dignity of the white-haired Elsa Moore stopped the two.

She stood slowly, stiff from sitting so long. For a second she struggled to obtain her balance.

Kathy pulled herself back onto the narrow bed. From a laceration just below her hairline, blood flowed in a crimson rivulet.

"Don't worry, Kathy." The old woman's voice was surprisingly strong as she turned to the girl she had only known for a short while. "Thank you for what you just did. I'll pray for you, my dear. You are a fine girl. As fine as any granddaughter."

She shuffled on tired legs toward the door, before the impatient guards could command her.

The door swung shut behind them.

Alone, Kathy O'Connor let the tears flow. Her thin shoulders shook with sobs as her past fears merged with present grief. Streams of red reached the line of her jaw, and she used the bottom of her T-shirt to dab at them. Finally, she held the bloodied tail of her shirt against the scalp wound; the laceration slowly stopped bleeding and clotting began. Still tear-bright, Kathy's brown eyes gazed across the room at nothing.

A resolve she did not know she possessed, a kind of resolve absent from her life until now, was beginning to form in her.

THE CIRCUITRY WITHIN THE MIND of Mack Bolan did its work. A subliminal piece of 35mm black-and-white film came to view on the screen inside his head. Seen only briefly during the course of some long-ago study of hundreds of similar photos, this one now came clear in the big guy's memory.

LeValle. Maurice LeValle. Suspected of aiding in the financing of a major hit in West Germany. Bolan observed him through the window at the north end of the laboratory. He was in urgent discussion with two others, a man and a woman.

LeValle. Suspected of providing the funds that went toward the purchase of explosives used against Jews living in Paris. Suspected of planning the kidnapping of half a dozen American executives in Bolivia less than a year ago. Suspected. Always suspected but never proved guilty because the dapper man in the expensive suits was too slippery ever to become exposed to risk.

The thin guy at LeValle's side was familiar to The Executioner only as a type. Through the window, Bolan felt the man's cunning and barely contained savagery. Yeah, a type all right. A type Bolan chewed up and spat out with zeal in the consecrated rage of his terrorist wars.

A door opened at the far end of the room. Two men escorted an elderly woman a few paces into the room and halted. Dwarfed by the two large guards, the old woman seemed terribly frail.

Bolan saw the female terrorist dismiss the guards with a wave of her hand. She turned to the man Bolan had pegged as LeValle and spoke rapidly. He could not hear the words. The old woman was glancing from one terrorist to the other with obvious interest.

The eye-catching younger woman poured some liquid into a glass. She picked up the glass and extended it toward the old woman.

The two females faced each other. Then,

with a look of mocking defiance, the old woman accepted the glass thrust toward her. Her bright birdlike eyes never left the cruel eyes of the woman in white, as she swallowed the liquid without hesitation.

Bolan felt the hair rise on the back of his neck.

Within seconds the drug did its work. The thin hand holding the glass contracted as though possessed of a will of its own. The glass shattered in her grasp. Shards of glass bit into paper-thin skin, slashed muscles and tendons.

Her face contorted. The old woman buckled, crumpled to the floor, the muscles in her crippled legs tightening as the drug did its work. The woman became a bundle of twisting flesh as violent convulsions took possession of her. The experiment had been deliberately compressed.

Though Bolan had viewed death many times, he had never seen terror so clearly etched in the very muscle tissue of its victim. The hideously foreshortened effect of the drug had destroyed her grotesquely.

He dropped to a crouch and soft-soled it down the length of the building.

Ten yards to his right a shadow detached

itself from a larger area of dark and moved toward him.

The Beretta chugged, and a silent slug slammed into the guard.

Bolan moved on, faster now.

13

JOSH WILLIAMS TURNED the tuning knob a fraction and listened intently. The headphones on his graying head emitted sounds that brought him no satisfaction. With an abrupt gesture he flipped a switch, draining the life from the extensive array of shortwave equipment before him. He pulled the headphones from his head and placed them on the table beside his station log.

"I don't know which gives me the greater satisfaction. A thirty-thousand-dollar radio that can't raise Aberdeen, Scotland, or a grandkid who's wearing a hole in the carpet with her pacing."

Sara turned to face her grandfather. "Sorry." She sipped a cup of coffee. "I've been thinking." She crossed to the kitchen and poured the cool black liquid into the sink. "It's late." She glanced at the watch on her slim wrist.

"You planning on turning in soon?" he asked.

"Not really. I thought I'd stay up for a while."

"Any objection to my keeping you company?" asked the old man.

"Not if you'll promise to put off that fence repair down by the creek for another day."

"You talked me into it," he agreed.

He rose from the straight-backed wooden chair and gave a disgusted look at the extensive radio setup. He moved to a body-worn platform rocker near the stone fireplace. Sara tossed a length of lodgepole pine into the glowing embers.

"Rate we're going we'll use up our winter's wood before winter gets here," Josh grumbled.

Sara ignored the remark as she curled her long legs beneath her on the carpet in front of the raised hearth. For minutes she let her eyes range around the room with its knotty pine interior and general evidence of domestic comfort.

"If you'd like," Josh said without preamble, "we could drive down toward Loveland and Fort Collins one of these days. Talk to a couple of those greyhound breeders I know.

Maybe persuade them to part with three or four pups that aren't up to setting track records. Save them the trouble of killing the dogs,'' he added as though the idea had just occurred to him.

"Thanks, Josh. That might be a good idea. But not too soon. Let's think about it."

At length he spoke again, giving vent to what was uppermost but unsaid in both their minds.

"My guess is John Phoenix is using his quiet shooting pistol on them. What do you think?"

"I think it was a silenced 9mm Beretta."

"Whatever, my dear, whatever. My bet is that John Phoenix is doing all right for himself."

Sara turned to face the old man. "I can hike down there alone. You can use the 4WD and cover me from the top of the ridge."

"And if you needed help I could just throw rocks at them from a distance of maybe half a mile."

She crossed to the gun cabinet with quick, impatient steps. Her slender fingers stroked the stock of her Winchester.

She spoke silently to herself. *Someone has to help him.*

14

SNATCHES OF ORDERS carried by the night air came to the ace death-dealer's ears.

"Infiltration."

"Perimeter breached."

"Find them!"

"Shoot to kill!"

KATHY RECOGNIZED the approaching steps and voices the instant they entered the building. Holbein's voice was familiar, hated. The other voice she had heard only minutes earlier when Lavinia and the two men had left the building. Kathy O'Connor held her breath as the footsteps neared her room.

Still motionless, not breathing, she watched in dread as the knob turned and the door swung inward.

She saw Maurice LeValle's smooth face, his possessive eyes, his slick suit.

"What happened to Mrs. Moore?" she yelled out. "Where is she?"

LeValle turned to Kurt.

"Do you mean the old woman who was with you?" Kurt asked Kathy.

The girl nodded angrily.

"She's just fine. She sends you her best wishes." Holbein's face showed some animation as he recalled the old woman's final seconds.

"She's dead, isn't she? You killed Mrs. Moore the same way you're killing everyone in here!"

"Enough of that." LeValle stepped forward. His right hand shot out. The sound of flesh striking flesh was like the report of a small-caliber revolver. Kathy recoiled. "We are having trouble in this operation, some nuisance at the moment. We may be attacked," said LeValle, breathing heavily. "I do not have the patience for your hysterics."

As he spoke, LeValle slipped free of his suit coat. "It is to your advantage to provide me with a pleasurable evening," he said quietly.

Maurice LeValle gave a sick grin in anticipation of the scene he knew would follow. It was going to be a hell of a night.

One hell of a night.

15

BOLAN BURST THROUGH THE DOOR like an avenging angel of death.

Lavinia Vitalli's dark eyes took in the terrifying image.

Bolan kept the muzzle of the Beretta trained on the woman like an all-seeing eye. She was the only one who remained in the room where the experiment had been done. The corpse of the old woman lay near his feet.

"Do you mind if I finish my wine?" Lavinia said with exalted sarcasm.

Her chill eyes settled on the glacial cold of Bolan's blue gaze. Not liking the compeition, she turned away.

With his free hand Bolan located the variable-frequency remote-control unit. He came up to her so she could see the device.

Bolan thumbed it.

He was rewarded with a muted explosion, a

flash in the window, a *whump* as the gas tank's in the motor pool ignited.

The muscles and cords in Lavinia's neck became rigid. The sounds were familiar to her as the stock in trade of terrorists the world over.

"You're too late." She spat the words across the space between them. "Kurt has already left. You cannot stop him now. And you are going to die, just like the others."

She hurled the wineglass at Bolan's face. His reflexes took over long before it reached him. Out of the corner of his eye he saw the glass sail past and smash into the wall.

Lavinia spun toward a weapon on a nearby table.

Bolan's Beretta whispered its statement.

A hole appeared in the white smock by her right breast.

The punch of the 9mm chunk of power had snapped her body back against the wall. Lavinia Vitalli now stared down in horrified fascination as the front of her smock was stained spreading scarlet.

She could not believe that her own body could be violated. The horror of it overwhelmed all pain.

Bolan, without anger, without triumph, stroked the autopistol's trigger again.

The second shot brought twin deaths. As Lavinia Vitalli died, with her died her dreams for conquest and domination.

The evil woman's body slipped to the floor as Bolan turned toward the door.

BOLAN CRASHED INTO THE CORRIDOR. With the 93-R at the ready, he glared down the long hallway.

Kurt Holbein skidded to a halt. For milliseconds stretching to eternity, the two men faced each other.

Bolan could all but see the workings of Holbein's mind.

Each hand held a glass-stoppered container. Holbein was about to make a life-or-death decision.

Bolan speeded up the process by making the choice for him.

A soft *phut* from the autopistol on single-shot shattered one of the two bottles. Shards of glass flew as the force of the 9mm slug exploded the container. Slivers of glass embedded themselves in Holbein's flesh.

The guy began to shake.

Each tiny shard of glass that had pierced Holbein's flesh had become a hypodermic needle injecting the killer liquid into the man's body.

Holbein's face became a contorted mask as muscles drew the surface flesh into grotesque agony.

The second container and its once-precious contents fell to the tile floor. In a spreading pool of liquid, the usefulness of the concoction evaporated, by the side of the man who had once been a greedy lover of power unlimited.

A twisted mouth struggled open to draw oxygen into lungs unable to expand.

Grim memories played in Bolan's mind, of his Japanese mission where the venomous toxins of terror had also crackled at his feet, just a step away from the realization of mass poisoning on an unspeakable level. Grim memories indeed, in a war everlasting.

Bolan sidestepped the writhing mass on the floor and moved down the corridor.

Autopistol extended and ready to cough death, the invader checked each door, alternating from one side of the corridor to the other. Each room was empty except for one or two narrow cots.

Empty except for the stench of fear and despair that clung to every wall.

Bolan heard a sound.

A girl's whimper.

He went through the door as though propelled from a catapult.

LeValle was in a partial crouch by the the bed, a hand on the leg of the seminaked girl who sat leaning back on her arms, her face a mask of terror-stricken resignation. A blood-stained T-shirt lay on the blanket beside her.

"Half time," the Executioner announced in the hard voice of death.

LeValle glared in mute reply. The girl gazed up at Mack Bolan. Life returned to her expression. The big warrior's face was hard, and yet it was a mask of righteous anger. This man in black was an avenging angel, not a vicious brute.

He had come not to ravage the defenseless, but to liberate the innocent and punish the guilty.

That is what she saw in his face.

"Listen," LeValle began slowly. "Killing me won't solve anything."

"It'll be a step in the right direction," Bolan said simply, aiming the Beretta at the guy's forehead.

Footsteps rang on the floor of the corridor. Bolan turned sharply to snap a glance in the direction of the noise. He saw a lone member of the terrorist guard force at the end of the hallway. The guy was gazing at the corpse of Kurt Holbein. He spotted the Executioner as well. The guard clawed open a button-flap holster on his hip and began to draw his side arm.

Bolan swung the Beretta in a single smooth motion and aimed with the speed and precision of one of the world's best combat shooters. The silenced 93-R hissed. A tongue of orange flame slashed out from the suppressor muzzle.

A 125-grain hollowpoint projectile split the bridge of the guard's nose. The guy's head recoiled. The back of his skull burst open. His body fell against the wall and smeared a trail of blood and brains as it slid to the floor.

Still on his knees, LeValle reached under the bunk for a 9mm Makarov in a gunbelt that he had removed from his thick waist before kneeling in front of the girl. It was the only move he could make that might save his corrupt life.

The bare-breasted girl suddenly sprung up from the mattress and whipped a bare knee into LeValle's face. The unexpected blow knocked the fat man backward into the cell wall. He snarled. In rage he threw himself at the girl.

She pivoted on one foot and launched a high sidekick. Bolan watched her long naked leg shoot out. The bottom of her foot smacked into LeValle's flabby chest and propelled the man into the wall once more.

"Bastard!" she screamed. "Pig! Son of a bitch!"

Bolan intended to pull her aside and get a clear shot at LeValle.

But the girl swung another lanky leg and threw a kick at LeValle's head. This time the fat man was ready for her. His hands caught her ankle and twisted it sharply. The girl was thrown off balance and collided into the Executioner.

Bolan caught the girl and swung her to the bunk. LeValle charged into the warrior before Bolan could use the Beretta. Both men staggered across the threshold of the cell into the corridor.

LeValle proved to be faster and stronger than his paunchy frame suggested. The terrorist rammed Bolan's back against the wall and seized the wrist of the Executioner's gun hand with both of his flabby hands.

Bolan slammed a knee into LeValle's gut.

The fat man merely grunted and gave Bolan's wrist a hard twist.

The Beretta slipped from Bolan's grasp.

The Executioner's free hand lashed a judo chop at LeValle's neck. The edge of his hand struck the terrorist in the cheekbone. LeValle responded by driving the point of an elbow into Bolan's solar plexus. Bolan's chest felt like it had exploded as the breath was forced from his lungs.

The girl rejoined the battle and attacked LeValle from behind, kicking him in the back of the knee. The cannibal king's leg buckled. The girl had caught him off guard before, so she no longer had that advantage. LeValle, still holding Bolan's forearm with one hand, whipped a vicious backhand to her face and knocked her back.

Bolan's arm broke free of LeValle's grip. His fist smashed into the side of the terrorist's jaw. The same fist opened and slashed a cross-body judo chop to LeValle's mouth. The blow split the fat man's lip and cracked the philtrum bone of his upper jaw. Bolan snap-kicked him in the crotch. LeValle's bloodied lips formed a compact oval as he convulsed in agony, spittle dripping from his mouth.

Bolan leaped at the dazed man, just as the girl launched another kick of her own, bringing her foot up under the guy's flapping arm. His radial bone snapped. LeValle opened his mouth to scream, but Bolan had seized his fleshy throat with his right hand in a "tiger mouth" grip that made speech impossible. His thumb and index finger pinched off LeValle's carotid arteries while the bent knuckle of his middle finger dug into the terrorist's windpipe.

LeValle struggled helplessly. Bolan immobilized the guy's left arm with a hammerlock and continued to throttle him. LeValle's eyes bulged. His tongue dangled from its gaping mouth.

A damp stain appeared at the crotch of LeValle's trousers. Bolan smelled the stink of urine and fear. He felt the man's body convulse in wave after wave of muscle spasms.

Finally LeValle quit moving. Bolan released him. The terrorist slumped to the floor, a lifeless lump of putrid flesh.

"Thank God you showed up," the girl gasped breathlessly. "Whoever you are."

"John Phoenix," Bolan replied. "What's your name?"

"Kathy," the girl said.

Bolan retrieved his Beretta 93-R and strode out to the body of the guard he had shot. Bolan found the dead man's gun, a Czech M1950. The small 7.65mm pistol was an inferior combat piece. Bolan ignored it and frisked the corpse. He found nothing save a wallet, keys and a walkie-talkie hooked to the guy's gunbelt.

Kathy joined the Executioner. She had found her torn T-shirt and held LeValle's Markarov pistol in her fist. Bolan nodded at the gun.

"You know how to use that?" he asked.

"A little," she admitted. "Not much."

"Then don't use it at all unless you absolutely have to," he told her. "And keep the safety on until you intend to shoot."

"Okay," Kathy said. "But how do we get past the guards outside?"

"We have to convince them to look the other way," Bolan replied.

16

THE EXECUTIONER AND KATHY moved from the cell to a shabby nearby office. A lamp on a battered metal desk supplied the only light. Bolan peered out of the window at the burning remnants of the motor pool. Terrorists darted across the parade field. The enemy was armed to the teeth.

"Now they know for sure that the compound has been penetrated," Bolan said with chill sarcasm.

"Then we're trapped," the girl groaned.

"You started fighting back tonight," the Executioner told her. "Don't stop now."

"Okay," Kathy managed a weak smile. "You don't need a quitter on your hands."

"A quitter is the only real loser in life," the big warrior stated. "And we are going to win."

"Muller!" a voice crackled from the floor

of the cell block corridor. "Come in, Muller. Over."

The girl gasped, but Bolan gave her hand a reassuring squeeze, firm yet gentle. He stepped into the corridor and knelt by the dead guard. The Executioner unhooked the guy's walkie-talkie from its belt.

"Muller?" the voice squawked from the transceiver. "Do you read me? Over. Muller?" the caller insisted.

Bolan pressed the transmit button. "Muller here," he grunted, scratching the mouthpiece with a thumbnail to simulate static and to distort his voice. "My talkie is on the fritz. Tried to contact you a minute ago. Over."

"Well, you've got me now," the voice replied. "Is everything okay over there? Need assistance? Over."

"Negative," Bolan said. "LeValle was pissed because I interrupted his fun. Can't believe that guy. Over."

"Didn't he even let you cop a feel?" the voice chuckled.

"Negative," the Executioner repeated. "But LeValle wants to know what the hell's gone wrong with our defenses."

"We'd like to know the same thing,"

growled the terrorist lieutenant. "But don't tell LeValle that."

"He's worried about the lab," Bolan told his "commander." "He called Lavinia Vitalli and got no answer. He wants a large unit of men to check the lab building immediately. Search top to bottom. We don't want a midnight shoplifter to get his hands on our wonder drugs. Over."

"I'll send a team pronto," the voice promised. "Already sent you some reinforcements just in case. Should be there any second. Over."

The Executioner sucked air through his teeth. He hit the transmit button. "Can't hurt, I guess," he told the guy. "Thanks. Over."

"Stay on your toes, Muller," the commander urged. "Over and out."

Bolan dropped the walkie-talkie. It bounced off the chest of its deceased owner. He turned to Kathy.

"Get behind the desk and stay down," he ordered, unsheathing his Beretta 93-R. "Company coming."

Seconds later, the barracks door burst opened and three young terrorists entered. They were not expecting trouble. Their weapons were still slung on their shoulders. One guy had put a cigarette in his mouth and was firing it with a plastic lighter. Another raised a walkie-talkie to his lips.

"Kassam here," the team leader spoke into the transceiver. "We're in position. Over."

"Dig in, Kassam!" the voice from the radio ordered. "We're at the lab. Lavinia is dead! The shit has hit the fan! Over!"

"I read you, Comrade. . ." Kassam said.

"You fucking well better! Over and out!"

Kassam growled a crude remark in his native tongue and attached the walkie-talkie to his belt. He turned to the two men under his command.

"Well, you guys heard—"

One of the flunkies snapped back his head as if about to nod vigorously. A mist of pink and gray brains gushed from behind his cranium and his body tilted back to crash to the floor.

Kassam heard the metallic burp of a silenced pistol and the grunt of pain and surprise from his other underling. A bullet had punched through the guy's left temple and sliced through his brain to pop out the right side of his head.

Bolan appeared from the mouth of the cell block, his Beretta held in a two-handed combat grip. To some observers, the sound-suppressor made the pistol look like a sci-fi laser blaster. Kassam was one of those. His eyes bugged from their sockets. He seized the pistol grips of the Soviet PPSh 41 machine gun that hung from its shoulder strap by his right hip.

The Executioner drilled him between the eyes with a 9mm slug.

"It's over," Bolan announced.

Kathy raised her head and peered over the top of the desk. "It's sure over for them," she whispered.

The Executioner moved to the window and eyeballed the laboratory building. Every light in the place was on. Figures of terrorist goons passed by windows as they searched the lab and its connected rooms. A jeep, probably the only vehicle that had not been destroyed when the motor pool blew up, was parked in the center of the parade field.

Three men rushed from the Land Rover to the door of the lab center where two terrorists waited for them. One guy held a walkie-talkie. Bolan wondered if he was the same guy he had spoken to a few minutes before.

The cannibals had congregated in a temple of evil to find their high priestess dead.

It was time for them to join her.

Bolan removed the remote-control detonator from his pocket and triggered the second button. The exploding plastique sounded like a large firecracker from Bolan's position. Then the blast ignited the chemicals in the lab. Potassium chlorate, magnesium sulfate, phosphoric acid and God knows what else, all erupted like a volcano within the lab.

Windows burst. Walls cracked open. Mangled, charred corpses hurtled from openings. Flames rose like skeletal fingers.

The terrorists in the doorway were hit by a blast of rolling fire. Clothing and hair ignited, skin charred to the bone. One ghastly figure staggered across the parade field. Enshrouded in flames, the hideous apparition stumbled several yards before it collapsed in a smouldering heap.

Disciples of destruction had become unhuman torches. Mack Bolan was purifying the evil in the laboratory with death itself. The roar of the death sentence and the crackle of its execution still filled their ears as they gazed out the window.

"My God!" Kathy exclaimed. "What was all that?"

"You'll see," Bolan replied.

He returned the Beretta 93-R to leather and gathered up the dead team leader's PPS subgun. One of the best of the Soviet-bloc small arms, the PPSh 41 is compact and dependable, weighing less than nine pounds, yet its banana magazine holds 35 rounds. The Russian SMG featured a sliding wire stock instead of the original solid one. The Ivans would not admit it, but they had gotten that innovation from the Chinese K-50M. The Chicoms, in turn, had copied the slide stock of a French MAT-49.

Bolan pulled back the bolt and made certain there was a round in the chamber of the PPS. Then he crept to the door, alone. The jeep was still intact. The Executioner and Kathy would ride out of the compound in style.

Two terrorists suddenly materialized from the shadows. They spotted Bolan's head and swung their Kalashnikov rifles at the invader. The Executioner was faster. He fired the PPS from the hip. A stream of 7.62mm rounds ripped into the pair before they could trigger their weapons. They performed an uncoordinated death dance before they fell dead to the ground.

A volley of full-auto projectiles chewed at the corner of the barracks near Bolan. He glimpsed four figures on the parade field as he ducked behind the building. What he had seen in that instant spelled big trouble.

Two of the terrorists were armed with AK-47s. The others were crouched by the jeep with grenades in their fists, about to pull the pins.

"Hold your fire!" Bolan yelled. *"I surrender!"*

The terrorists did not reply. They did not lob the grenades either. Bolan had bought a few seconds.

"I'm going to throw out my gun," Bolan called out. "Just don't shoot me!"

He turned to Kathy, who stood trembling in the doorway. He pointed at the corpses sprawled on the office floor.

"Take one of those guns and throw it through the window," he instructed. "Fast!"

The girl stripped an assault rifle from a dead man's shoulder and hurled it at the window. Glass and the wooden framework shattered. The AK-47 fell to the ground in full view of the men by the jeep.

If the tactic worked, the terrorists would be

distracted, their attention drawn away from Bolan's position. If it had not worked, the Executioner would find out soon enough.

He leaped from the cover of the barracks and dropped to one knee, training the PPS on the four confused savages. The Russian SMG snarled as Bolan swept the weapon in a steady left-to-right motion to spray the terrorists with 7.62mm destruction.

Bodies hopped and jerked from the impact of multiple bullets crashing into flesh. One of the goons yanked the pin from his grenade as he fell against the jeep. The hand-bomb exploded. Bolan dived for cover as the blast battered the Land Rover and shredded the terrorists with shrapnel.

Two long shapely legs appeared above the Executioner's head as he lay prone on the ground. Kathy helped him to his feet and asked if he was hurt.

"I'm okay," Bolan assured her. "But our ride was cancelled. We'll have to hoof it."

They moved through the compound, running behind the cover of billets buildings. The fires in the motor pool and lab continued to burn. Flickering yellow light flooded the installation. The only sounds were the crackle of flames and their own racing heartbeats. No voices cried out. No shots were fired.

Had Bolan wiped out the terrorist vermin?

The answer appeared abruptly. An enemy gunman darted from the corner of a billets, a Skorpion machine pistol in his fists. The Czech mini-blaster spat a volley of 7.65mm rounds at him and Kathy.

Bolan hit the dirt, pulling the girl down as he dropped to the ground. Bullets sizzled overhead like a swarm of metallic hornets. Bolan returned fire, shooting with one hand from a prone stance, the wire stock of the PPS jammed against his shoulder.

He emptied the banana clip into the terrorist. The man's body seemed to leap from view as if yanked backward by invisible wires.

The report of pistol shots cracked behind Bolan. He rolled quickly, discarding the empty PPS to claw at the AutoMag on his hip.

Kathy held the Markarov in her fists, and she was repeatedly pulling the trigger.

The girl pumped round after round into the thrashing figure of a terrorist gunman who had appeared from the opposite end of the billets.

The enemy had tried to get them in a cross-fire ambush. The tactic may have succeeded if

Kathy had not checked behind them as Bolan was taking care of the first assailant.

Kathy fired the last 9mm from the Markarov and the slide locked open on the empty chamber. She dropped the gun and stared at the pulverized corpse of the man she had shot to pieces. Bolan took her hand.

"You didn't take his life," the Executioner told her. "You saved ours."

He moved to the man he had blasted with the PPS. A stray bullet had damaged the breech of the Skorpion machine pistol. The weapon was unreliable, so Bolan left it. He found two Russian F-1 hand grenades hooked to the dead man's webbing. The F-1 ressembled the old Mark 11A1 "pineapple," with a metal stem jutting from the serrated body. Bolan had handled such grenades back in Nam. He took the blasters and returned to Kathy.

"One more lap to go," he told her.

They jogged to the last billets, less than ten yards from the main gate. Bolan scanned the area for enemy forces.

He yanked the pin from an F-1 and tossed the grenade at the gate. It exploded. The gate trembled violently and dangled on broken hinges. Bolan lobbed the other Russian pineapple. The second blast sent the gate crashing to the ground.

"Now!" he shouted. "Double time!"

Bolan and the young girl dashed for the opening. An autoweapon snapped flame as a wounded terrorist limped after them, firing an AK with one hand. The other hand been amputated by flying shrapnel.

Bolan hurled his last grenade, an American M-26 fragger. It exploded with monstrous force, tearing the lone terrorist limb from limb.

The tactic was overkill, but it was meant to encourage any other survivors to keep their heads down long enough to allow Bolan and Kathy to reach the gate. The tactic worked.

The Executioner and his female ally ran across the fallen barricade. They were finally out of the terrorist compound and into the meadow.

Perhaps, at last, the Rocky Mountains nightmare was over.

17

WHEN RAUL HERNANDEZ SPOKE to his second-in-command he slowed his speech automatically, allowing a fractional pause to separate each word.

"No attackers will leave this valley alive. Not one!"

"Of course."

"Check out the 4WD hidden in the reserve area and make certain it is functional. It is our only vehicle. Lock in the hubs. Check the .30-caliber, and get it into its mounts on the cab. Remain with the truck. Listen for me on channel three."

When Raul said no more, the second-in-command turned on the heel of his polished boot and double-timed it to the reserve area.

If Raul said no one was to leave the valley alive, then no one would leave it alive. There was no question in his mind.

VIETNAM! Grim memories flooded Bolan's fading consciousness. A red yellow flash had erupted only yards from the fleeing pair. The murderous blast had filled the air with steel the size of ball bearings. Antipersonnel landmine!

The shock of the radio-detonated claymore's bellyful of destruction numbed his mind. But the shrapnel that had torn through his right calf muscle shook his dazed consciousness awake.

Bolan saw that Kathy too had been hit.

He rose to his feet and dragged Kathy with him. He willed the girl upright as much by his mind as by the pressure of his hand.

Hot steel had bored into her. Not knowing how badly Kathy was hit, knowing his own right leg was now less than fifty percent effective, Bolan's drive to continue was halted.

"It hurts," Kathy said. Her tone was fatalistic.

"We'll live!" Mack Bolan said. Everything depended on the will to survive.

Bolan saw the spreading stain on the left shoulder of the girl's T-shirt. It looked low enough to have missed the collarbone, high enough not to have damaged ribs.

Bolan decided to push onward, not stand and fight against unknown odds.

With legs pumping unevenly and lungs working like a pair of tortured bellows, Bolan limped on. Kathy was draped around his left shoulder. The AutoMag was drawn and leading the way.

Every time his damaged leg reached out and touched down, he feared it might betray him and buckle. Yet with each stride the leg held, despite the jolts of electric-hot pain traveling the length of it.

Together the slender girl and the tall, powerful man staggered into the night while behind them the muffled sound of the engine of a 4WD roared to life.

Their pursuers had already detonated the mine; now they were set to chew up the meat.

18

SLIPPING AND SLIDING, Josh followed his granddaughter down the wooded slope. For the third time in less than a minute he caught a boot toe on a fallen branch and lurched forward.

"You all right, Josh?" she called.

"About as okay as a man can be when he's just run head-on into a lodgepole."

Sara moved ahead. Through the maze of tree trunks and branches ahead and below, she could see the glow of the inferno blazing within the compound.

Puffing and wheezing, Josh reached her side.

"You going to spend all night standing here enjoying the view? Maybe you think that Winchester of yours is head-shot accurate at this distance...."

"Isn't it?" Without awaiting his reply Sara plunged ahead. Knowing that the combination of distance and darkness made their efforts all but hopeless, yet determined beyond measure to do something, anything, Sara blindly ate up ground.

AT HIS SIDE, Kathy continued to match his speed. When Bolan veered from the road the girl stumbled, but his powerful arm refused to let her body lose balance.

Blood flowed freely from their wounds. Each step was a lesson in pain.

Behind them the roaring of the heavy 4WD came closer with every second.

Suddenly a probing finger of white light slashed from the side of the truck as the driver activated the spotlight.

Desperately Bolan tried to pick up the pace. He kept their course straight. There would be time enough to waste energy by dodging and darting once the light located them.

The big .44 was a match for most hardguys at up to a hundred yards. Bolan sought a rock outcrop or even a depression where he could launch his counterattack. Knock out the driver, then deal with foot soldiers when and if they closed the gap....

Kathy caught a sneakered toe on a small

rock and fell headlong. She pulled the big guy in a swinging arc that brought him around to face the oncoming truck.

The truck's .30-caliber fired a dozen rounds of belt-fed as a range check. The incoming slugs chewed the mountain meadow a scant half dozen yards behind where Bolan was pulled up at bay.

Kathy's commands came in choppy bursts. "Leave me. Go on. I can't get up. Go on." She struggled for breath. Her wound and the long run had taken their inevitable toll. For the shaking girl at his feet the end was at hand.

Bolan went into two-handed combat stance. The big .44 came on target, steadied, and roared.

The shot smashed into the truck's windshield, inches to the right of the driver's head. Though bits of glass peppered his face and neck, the zombie driver did not react. The truck continued its relentless plunge across the meadow.

AWARE THAT TIME WAS UP, Sara stopped on the top side of a length of substantial deadfall. By the time Josh joined her she had the little .243 Winchester 70 tight against her shoulder as she sought to make sense of the scene below through the K6 scope.

"That fire give any backlight?" Josh's words were clear though his lungs worked double time to supply him with oxygen.

"It helps." Sara continued to search the area in front of the oncoming 4WD where she had noticed a flash of T-shirt and bare legs. If the girl's skin had not been exposed and her shirt had got a little dirtier, Sara would never have seen the pair.

As she brought the fallen girl into view, a muzzle-flash flickered on her scope lens.

"He's shooting at the truck."

The .30 caliber chattered some blind rounds as the light reflected the truck's swerve.

Bolan's big .44 roared again. This time Sara caught the flash as she worked to bring the oncoming vehicle into her cross hairs.

Using the driver-side headlight as her point of reference, she elevated the rifle until she estimated she had the driver's torso as her target. Her slender forefinger tightened and the .243 responded.

Sara squeezed off a second round, then a third.

Hounded by the 100-grain rain, the truck went into a power slide.

BOLAN'S REACTION WAS IMMEDIATE. He bent, scooped the shaking girl into his arms and turned toward the woods as the truck came to a sideways stop.

Kathy sobbed brokenly, trying unsuccessfully to still the shaking of her shoulders. Carefully but without ceremony, Bolan dumped the girl to the ground, then put a dozen paces between her and himself. He went prone and used both hands to steady the .44.

Four times Bolan's trigger finger tightened, sending destruction into the side of the vehicle.

Sara, aware of the unusual calm she experienced in her vantage spot, triggered more 100-grains into the stricken vehicle. One of her efforts caused Gino Cabelli to bow out of this life in a mist of head gore.

Whether it was the AutoMag or the Winchester made no difference: a chunk of metal tore its way through the thin skin of the truck's reserve fuel tank.

Nearly empty, the reserve tank was filled with explosive fumes.

Friction from the passage of the spinning slug did what was necessary.

The vehicle erupted in a punishing blast.

Seconds later the main tank became a gushing fountain of fire.

Thrown free when the truck began its slide, Raul Hernandez was showered with a liquid blaze that engulfed him and turned his life into blazing pain.

19

TWICE JOSH STUMBLED AND FELL. Each time the girl he held in his arms moaned softly but bit back any outcry.

Sara supported a portion of Bolan's weight as the quartet made its way up the steep hillside toward the Williamses' 4WD.

"We'll make it, child. Just keep hanging on," wheezed the old man, "and I'll try and stop stumbling and falling about like the old fool that I am."

Kathy's indistinct reply was lost to Bolan; Josh's boots had dislodged a stream of loose rock. At eleven thousand feet, conversation was not always possible as their lungs sought oxygen to offset their burdens, and their pain.

Josh crested the top of the ridge. He stood with Kathy in his arms, briefly outlined against the night sky that would soon show signs of dawn.

"Made it here!" They had reached the old man's vehicle. Within minutes the four mountain warriors were aboard and settled.

Bolan supported Kathy's head on his shoulder during the bone-jarring drive down the sloping back of the mountain. The trail, obvious only to Josh and perhaps Sara, took them in a circuitous route that seemed never-ending. Eventually the tough vehicle emerged onto a gravel road.

Bolan felt Kathy's forehead. It was warm to the touch.

By the time the high-riding vehicle drew to a halt before the mountain ranch house, the girl's teeth were chattering despite her best efforts to stop them.

At Sara's direction Bolan supported Kathy long enough for Josh to scramble around the front of the truck.

"I've got her."

Wordlessly Bolan released his hold on the girl.

THE SPACIOUS KITCHEN became the scene of immediate medical and recuperative activity. Within minutes Sara was ready to begin work.

Kathy's T-shirt parted as Sara slid a pair of

scissors up the length of the garment. With professional skill she eased the bloodied cloth away from the raw wound.

"You're lucky. It passed through."

In a soothing tone, Sara told the girl what she was doing step by step.

"These injections are for local pain. But when I begin to clean the wound, it's still going to hurt. John will hold your shoulder still."

Pain-dulled brown eyes looked from Sara to Bolan. Wordlessly the girl nodded her acceptance.

"Josh, hand me the things as I call for them."

Kathy's breath hissed through clenched teeth as Sara delved with the medicated swab beyond the point the local had reached. When, with brutal efficiency, she forced the medicated swab through the girl's shoulder, Kathy O'Connor gave way to the pain and screamed in anguish.

Fifteen minutes later Mack Bolan ground his own teeth as a similar operation was performed on his leg.

"Curse and swear if it will help," Sara suggested.

"I'll spare you any noise," Bolan smiled grimly. "But I feel it, believe me."

"I don't have the facilities to do this properly, but what I've done is effective. You won't lose your leg to blood poisoning." Sara hesitated, then added, "I suspect you're the type that needs to keep moving."

Their eyes met and locked for seconds.

"You're a very resourceful person," Bolan said finally. "I owe you."

He moved slowly around the big room in a test of his bandaged leg. Then he asked the whereabouts of the telephone.

"Sorry, John," said Josh, "I don't have one. Blasted lines were always down. But I do have that ham radio rig over there. Want to check it out?"

Bolan followed the old fellow to the radio table in a dark corner of the room. Bolan surveyed the amateur's equipment for long seconds before turning to Josh.

"I reckon you'll want to talk privately," said the old man.

"Josh, I doubt that I could even turn that thing on."

"Give me some numbers," Josh said. His gnarled fingers moved over the bank of knobs and dials.

Bolan gave out a series. Within seconds the

voice of April Rose came clearly into the room.

"Striker here," Bolan identified himself into the mike.

"It's good to hear from you," glowed the woman's warm voice at the other end.

"Good here too. I'm finished in Paradise, lovely lady. I could use a ride out."

"Same place for pickup as for arrival?"

Bolan caught Josh's eye.

"How do you plan on leaving?" asked the old man.

"By helicopter."

"Yeah, figures. Well, if your pilot is worth anything, I've got an open pasture just below the house. We can bring him in with lights."

Bolan nodded his thanks. To April he said, "Tell Jack I'll be in an open area due north of target and south by west from the original landing site. Let's say forty minutes from now."

"Consider it done. Welcome back in advance, Mack."

Bolan signed off, then turned to look at Kathy. She sat at the hearth, holding a cup of hot chocolate; she was wrapped in a flannel robe whose better days were years in the past.

"I reckon maybe Kathy will be good company for Sara,'' Josh said, as if in response to Bolan's unspoken concern. "Kid looks as though she could do with some mountain air and good food."

Bolan questioned the girl by raising his eyebrows. Her smile was fleeting but it spoke volumes.

Bolan turned to Josh.

"It's just possible people may be asking you questions about me."

"Questions are cheap," muttered the old man amiably. "It's the answers that may be hard to come by."

Sara's expression indicated her agreement.

"They may insist," Bolan prodded.

Josh shot a glance at the fully stocked gun cabinet. "Not many call me a liar on my own land."

Bolan surveyed the young girl at the hearth. It was time to go. There was nothing to be gained by staying.

Josh caught the silent cue. "Best we go on down and make sure everything's ready." He reached for his Remington. "Just in case any of those coyotes are out and about." He moved toward the door.

Sara stepped toward Bolan. Her hand was warm in his. "Take care, John." Without awaiting his response, she pulled his head gently toward hers. Her lips were feather light on his cheek. Tears glistened in her eyes. For seconds she held onto the big guy, Then she let her arm drop from around his muscular neck.

Sara's expression revealed sadness at what might have been, at the enjoyments foregone by an attractive woman whose real beauty was in her independence and aloneness.

Bolan smiled a farewell to young Kathy, then turned and, without looking back, followed old Josh Williams into the remains of night.

Already the black was turning to silver gray with the promise of a new day to come.

"The only true morality is survival."
—*Robert Heinlein*

"A handgun is a truer friend
than a Swiss bank account."
—*Carl Lyons*

"Truth is my highest goal—to do what is good
and true—but the way to that goal is a low road
of hellfire that I must endure again and again.
And I will have it no other way, if the lowest
road allows for the survival of life at its best."
—*Mack Bolan*

Don Pendleton's

MACK BOLAN

THE EXECUTIONER SERIES

"Mack Bolan is constantly challenged and forever under pressure, but at all times he commands. There is no time or circumstance to permit life's luxuries for this man. Everything is transmuted in the fires of Bolan's world to focus in a white-hot spot upon the desperate situations always surrounding him. Bolan has supreme command, and I have known such men in real life."

—Don Pendleton

Pendleton's kind of man makes up the Gold Eagle squad of writers and researchers who are now working with him to ensure a new Bolan, as well as an Able Team or Phoenix Force adventure, every month of the year. It is an immense task for the creative team, and a commanding one for Don. But the call for new titles has become so great that Mack

Bolan's creator needs the very best backup available.

The Gold Eagle team of specialists has produced most of the Executioner titles in recent years, and Don Pendleton says its members have done "a beautiful job, producing classic Bolan adventures: multi-dimensional, well-structured and compelling. We have hellfire, and terror turned against terror, and very suspenseful writing that just sings from the pages."

This is an exciting development for Don Pendleton after years of single-handedly writing bestselling books, and it guarantees that his unique talent in the heroic-adventure genre (which he invented) will grow and flourish through the medium of the other energetic talents on the team. Gold Eagle's commitment is Don's commitment to provide only the very best.

"He freshens all the oldest words with all his blood," says Don of his leading character, Mack Bolan, a.k.a. Colonel John Phoenix. Bolan knows that the Stony Man team stands for the sanctity of life and that his enemies do not. Bolan's task is clear: "I have the tools, I have the ability, I am obligated." Bolan is in an enviable position for all men in that he knows the way "to be" is "to do." All of Bolan's men—and Pendleton's men—will do the job right, to the very best of their ability.

The Executioner is ready and willing to spend his blood, and that of his enemies, to freshen those old words: peace, justice and virtue.

The Executioner and his men are prepared to put the meaning back into those hallowed words.

With all their blood.

"Rocking action, explosive scenes, hard-hitting dialogue. Mack Bolan is great reading!"
—*New Breed*

MACK

THE EXECUTIONER 55

BOLAN

appears again in
Paradine's Gauntlet

APRIL ROSE WAS AT THE WHEEL of Mack's new battle cruiser, the Laser Wagon. The vehicle was stacked with the latest laser weaponry and optics; it had a weaponsmith's workshop in the living quarters at the rear. But still April was nervous.

She checked the time on the chronometer console in front of her. She bit her lip pensively. A weapon lay across her lap. Although she was piloting an RV masterpiece that its aerospace designers had dubbed the ultimate terrain module, she knew that when it came to actual war the gun was everything...and wheels were just wheels.

She slowed slightly. With her left hand she felt the gun in her lap for reassurance.

The American 180 automatic carbine was something special. Deceptively light, the rifle held 177 rounds of .22 hollowpoint ammunition in a drum mounted flat atop the slim receiver. In full automatic mode, the gun could generate a cyclic rate of 1800 rounds per minute, shredding human targets with grisly efficiency. A "Laser Lok" sight, mounted horizontally beneath the barrel, would eliminate the need to sight or aim, making any miss a virtual impossibility at a range of 200 yards or more.

And she would need the firepower, every ounce of it, to back up Bolan in his meeting with that deadly parasite called Paradine.

As she reached the corner, she heard the noise. Rounding the corner, she saw it. A vicious street fight. She parked and was EVA in seconds.

A pitched battle had broken out in the street directly in front of the Café Vittorio.

A dozen snipers had the restaurant beseiged. They poured autofire through the shattered windows.

Then April saw Mack Bolan. He was advancing under fire, squeezing off short, selective bursts from his machine pistol. Gunners on the street were taking cover, dodging into doorways of adjacent shops or crouching be-hind parked cars.

April snapped the autocarbine to her shoulder. She let the laser beam reach out and find the target. At one hundred yards the red spot was two inches wide and centered underneath a sniper's outstretched arm. It reminded April of a scarlet bull's-eye emblazoned on a target silhouette.

She stroked the trigger, ripping off a dozen rounds in half a second. There was no recoil, merely a sensation of the rifle's power, and the hollowpoint manglers were right on target, chewing flesh and vital organs into bloody pulp. The guy dropped his rifle and tumbled backward.

April dropped her sights and scanned for another target. She picked out a rifleman emerging from the doorway of a clothing store. The laser death-beam settled on his upper lip, and she held the trigger down for a full second. She watched face and skull disintegrate into a crimson spray.

A handgunner had her spotted and was swinging onto target acquisition when she hit him with a burst that tore his arm off at the shoulder.

A screech of brakes alerted her to sudden

danger at her back. April Rose spun around to find a dark sedan almost upon her, doors swinging open and disgorging troops. Half a dozen hardmen were closing on her, pistols cocked and ready.

She swung the 180 up and into action, brought the blinding laser beam into the nearest gunner's eyes. Before he could react, the bullets followed, drilling through his face and forehead, the impact lifting him completely off his feet and slamming him against the car.

And she held the trigger down, raking on across the car from left to right, watching tiny holes appear in doors and windshield. Startled troops were ducking, scrambling for cover; one of them, a shade too slow, was blown away and out of frame.

Pistols were cracking at her. Frighteningly close bullets whined past her.

She felt a stunning blow against her side, followed immediately by searing pain.

She was losing balance, falling, the auto-carbine spinning from her grasp.

MACK SAW APRIL ROSE STAGGER and fall. He saw the blood, bright and terrible, spread across the fabric of her battlesuit. . . .

An excerpt from

SOBs:

THE BARRABAS RUN
Coming soon from
Gold Eagle Books

THE STRAPS of Sylvia Powers's dress were hanging around her shoulders in shreds when they came out of the elevator.

"Damn, I guess I pushed the right button," she gasped, fumbling for her keys.

"Yeah, white squaw, I guess you did."

And she did. Even Billy Two couldn't explain it. He'd put the twenty grand into the back of his head in favor of making it with this woman.

Sylvia strode regally into the suite, mustering an awesome amount of dignity considering her state of disarray, and addressed her maid.

"Louella, I would like you to...."

"Yes, Mrs. Powers, I know. I'm going." She'd seen it all before.

"Cute little maid," Billy Two said, letting his juices flow now.

"Forget *her*! I was the one who pushed your button, remember?"

"Oh, yeah, woman, I remember."

"Jesus, you ignoble savage, take it easy!"

But the blood of his ancestors was boiling in Billy Two now. She became a captured squaw on the Mohawk Trail, part of the booty of war to a renegade Sioux.

He tore at her clothes.

"Billy, calm down a little...Billy...!"

Then he tore at his clothes.

"Billy...oh my God!"

Then he tore at her, digging into her, driving furious lunges that sent her mind soaring into space to look back in awe as her body was ravaged. She clutched at him, urged him on. He held her throbbing body against him and impaled her to the verge of complete surrender. He slackened his pace slightly and then drove forward again, full force.

She uttered a wailing cry. Her hair danced on the pillow, then her head tilted back as her body arched in a taut bow. She yielded to him. Then at last they let their muscles slacken.

"Good Lord, how the hell did we ever manage to take the country away from you people?" she managed to gasp.

"Too much fightin'. . . not enough lovin'," Billy panted.

"How much you say these boats will cost?"

"How much you got?"

"No, we don't play it that way with my cash. You name it."

"Twenty grand ought to do it."

"You got it. C'mere."

"Wait a minute, I gotta make a phone call." Billy extracted himself from the clawing tentacles of her arms and legs and padded back into the living room.

He called the bar and had Alex paged.

"Yeah?"

"Alex, it's me. We're in."

"In what?"

"In business, you asshole. You should have seen me; I was magnificent. We got twenty grand."

"Oh, yeah. Well, forget it."

The walls turned red. The phone turned red. The inside of Billy's eyeballs turned red.

"Forget it. *Forget it!* You slimy worm, you—"

"Easy, Billy, easy. We got a better deal. . . something with more security. Something worthwhile. You said you wanted to do something worthwhile."

Billy calmed down. Sylvia had entered the room. She was rubbing against him. He pushed her away.

"You remember a guy in Nam...Barrabas, Colonel Nile Barrabas?"

Billy thought. "Yeah, I think he's that crazy colonel that lead the raid into North Nam and freed all the airmen."

"That's him. He's down here in the bar with me now."

"So what?"

"Billy, he made us an offer."

"What kind of an offer?"

"One we can't refuse."

Now BARRABAS ran his hand over the folder of names. Yes, this crew could do anything. Vibrations of excitement slithered through his body and exploded in tiny bursts of anticipation in his brain. What was it Patton had said? "It's good we don't have a perpetual war. We'd grow to love it."

The men were hired like any other mercenary unit, with their allegiance totally to Barrabas. It was Barrabas who would supply the pro-American vision; therefore, should any of his men be captured, they could reveal nothing more than that they belonged to an

American mercenary unit whose leader was fanatic in his desire to wage a one-man campaign to further his nation's interests. Thus the government would never be implicated.

To further aid in secrecy, Barrabas had arranged that the group function like any other mercenary army. They were hired *on contract*. The price? Determined by Barrabas and nonnegotiable for each particular mission. The Soldiers of Barrabas were to handle all aspects of the mission themselves, through normal black-market channels, and with normal illicit arms.

They were an independent army, and only Barrabas knew the true nature of their existence.

The final security measure was that only he knew the identities of his men. As civilians to society and family alike, they had simply dropped off the face of the earth.

"Drink?" Barrabas pointed to the bottle of brandy. The arms dealer seated across from him declined, patting his stomach with a bony hand. "I've given it up. Age and the pressures of business."

"I've heard business was booming."

"Oh, it is, it is," Brooker said. "But mostly the heavy stuff. A little operator like me?

Well...." He left it hanging and slid back into the chair. "What can I do for you?"

"I've got a war."

Brooker looked at him long and hard, then looked at the floor. "AR-15s, jungle-greens with full packs, M-79s, side arms...that's what you're talking about."

"I need the firepower."

"Would you settle for .30s instead of 60s for the machine guns? Hard to locate right now."

"As long as they have mounts."

"Can do," Brookler mused, then looked at him directly again. "Sounds like a bush operation. Going to tell me?"

Barrabas shook his head. "Add Armalites to the list."

The dealer shrugged. "It's your money. A week?"

"Day after tomorrow."

"Not much notice, Nile. My suppliers...."

"Can you do it?"

"I think so."

THE MEN ARRIVED and settled in quickly. Everyone was on time, except Billy Two. He was six hours late because he'd been romancing "the most fascinating curves in this whole city."

O'Toole straightened him out quickly. "Was it good lad? Was it really good?"

The little man smiled and rolled back his dark eyes up into his head. "Good? It was fantastic!"

"That's great," O'Toole said, "because the SOBs don't have no court-martial or captain's mast or brig time for guys that screw up. All we got,¹ Billy, is your paycheck. I'm glad that piece of ass was good, because it just cost you two thousand bucks."

Everyone got the picture real quick.

THE BATTLE WAS INCREDIBLE. Vince had to make one of the more creative landings in the history of helicopter flight. Armalite fire had sliced back and forth beneath them as he anxiously waited to land, his touchdown options crumbling as the final moments of the firefight below bled the last ounce from the urge to seek and destroy. But he made it.

The copter vibrated on its sleds as the pilot stared in horror at the scene around him. Bodies were splayed across guns on both sides of the trench. Many were moaning, from a kneecap blown away or a stomach hanging open or an empty sleeve hanging where an arm had been.

Billy came running up. "Better get the Doc over here," he shouted, pointing to an outcrop across the clearing. "Emilio's been hit, bad. I think he's had it."

Billy looked around from the vantage point of the helicopter. The rotorwash blew his hair back. "Jesus," he said. "I'd almost forgotten what war was like. . . ."

SOBs : available soon from Gold Eagle.

An excerpt from

DAGGER:

THE CENTAUR CONSPIRACY

Coming soon from
Gold Eagle Books

THE CREEP WAS stumbling toward the open cabin now, hands reaching for the detonator.

Dagger clenched his teeth, twisted onto his right hip, and kicked him in the neck. The guy fell forward, his head cracking into the boat's steering wheel, his hand accidentally shoving the gear lever.

Suddenly the engine whined at a high pitch and the boat began to strain against the ties. It rocked in the water as it tried to pull free from the dock.

Dagger sprang to his feet, but too late. His enemy held the detonator. The guy stood crouching on the flybridge, a triumphant smile on his lips as he clutched the black box to his chest. His breathing was labored and two of his front teeth were newly chipped.

"If you press that," Dagger said, "you'll be destroying $6 million for your cause."

The man laughed, but it turned into a

choke. "You people will never change. Money is easy to get in this world, my friend. What is important is that Centaur's hostages in that other boat are going to die. That will fill the American people and their allies with fear. Bend them just a little more our way. Make our logic a little easier to accept."

The boat began to pull even harder against the dock. The sounds of splintering wood echoed across the water.

"Then let me put it another way," Dagger said. "If you press that I'll kill you."

The enemy laughed again, then looked deeper into Dagger's eyes. The laughter stopped. He snarled once and held out the detonator, his finger moving toward the button.

"Hey, you men," someone shouted from another boat further down the dock. "I don't care if you two get drunk and beat each other to hell and back. But goddamn it you're pulling the whole damn dock with you."

When his adversary snapped a glance at the dock, Dagger jumped forward and tried to grab the detonator. The guy saw the movement and stepped backwards. But he stepped back too far and flipped over the rail, grabbing desperately at Dagger and pulling him over too. They fell the ten feet onto the deck below and landed in a tangle of crushed arms and bruised legs. Dagger hit the deck with his wounded left arm and felt the nausea bubble into his throat.

The detonator had fallen out of the enemy's hand as they hit the deck, and it clattered to the back of the boat against the transom. Both men, still dazed from the fall, lurched after it.

The other guy reached it first.

Dagger was there a split second later, using what little strength he had left to swing a rocketing uppercut into the bastard's chin. The guy sprawled backwards, still holding the detonator. Dagger reached for it.

But too late.

His enemy pressed the button and the explosion across the bay lit up the sky in a celebration of destruction. The other boat fired wood and metal scrap thirty feet into the air. The flaming debris showered nearby. There were horrified screams amidst the orange crackling flames.

Dagger looked at the calm smile of fulfillment on the killer's face and felt his own body tighten. The straining boat rocked furiously now and part of the dock had already been torn away. The murderer's sweat-and-blood-smeared face glistened in the light of the distant fires. His smile broadened. "We win," he said. "We always win."

At that moment, the rest of the dock ripped free and the boat lurched forward, throwing Dagger off his feet. He landed on his wounded shoulder this time. But the other man was not so lucky. The boat's sudden thrust sent him somersaulting backwards over the transom.

And into the churning propellers.

His horror-filled scream sliced the cool night as no scream had ever done before. Dagger rushed to the edge of the boat. The guy's hands gripped the lacquered wood of the transom, but the lower half of his body was caught in the grinding T/233 MerCruiser propellers. The sea boiled a bloody red foam around his waist.

His face was twisted in agony as he struggled to pull what was left of his ravaged body from the water. Dagger reached down to grab his hands, but they were already slipping away.

The doomed man screamed again, looked over his shoulder, saw his own sneakered foot float by. Horror clenched his face and he let go of the boat.

Dagger watched his enemy disappear under the black water and for a moment he thought he saw a serpent from Hell glow hideously in the deep.

DAGGER: available soon from Gold Eagle.

HE'S EXPLOSIVE.
HE'S UNSTOPPABLE.
HE'S MACK BOLAN!

He learned his deadly skills in Vietnam...then put them to use by destroying the Mafia in a blazing one-man war. Now **Mack Bolan** is back to battle new threats to freedom, the enemies of justice and democracy—and he's recruited some high-powered combat teams to help. **Able Team**—Bolan's famous Death Squad, now reborn to tackle urban savagery too vicious for regular law enforcement. And **Phoenix Force**—five extraordinary warriors handpicked by Bolan to fight the dirtiest of anti-terrorist wars around the world.

Fight alongside these three courageous forces for freedom in all-new, pulse-pounding action-adventure novels! Travel to the jungles of South America, the scorching sands of the Sahara and the desolate mountains of Turkey. And feel the pressure and excitement building page after page, with nonstop action that keeps you enthralled until the explosive conclusion! Yes, Mack Bolan and his combat teams are living large...and they'll fight against all odds to protect our way of life!

Now you can have all the new Executioner novels delivered right to your home!

You won't want to miss a single one of these exciting new action-adventures. And you don't have to! Just fill out and mail the coupon following and we'll enter your name in the Executioner home subscription plan. You'll then receive four brand-new action-packed books in the Executioner series every other month, delivered right to your home! You'll get two **Mack Bolan** novels, one **Able Team** and one **Phoenix Force.** No need to worry about sellouts at the bookstore...you'll receive the latest books by mail as soon as they come off the presses. That's four enthralling action novels every other month, featuring all three of the exciting series included in The Executioner library. Mail the card today to start your adventure.

FREE! Mack Bolan bumper sticker.

When we receive your card we'll send your four explosive Executioner novels and, absolutely FREE, a Mack Bolan "Live Large" bumper sticker! This large, colorful bumper sticker will look great on your car, your bulletin board, or anywhere else you want people to know that you like to "Live Large." And you are under no obligation to buy anything—because your first four books come on a 10-day free trial! If you're not thrilled with these four exciting books, just return them to us and you'll owe nothing. The bumper sticker is yours to keep, FREE!

Don't miss a single one of these thrilling novels...mail the card now, while you're thinking about it. And get the Mack Bolan bumper sticker FREE!

BOLAN FIGHTS AGAINST ALL ODDS TO DEFEND FREEDOM!

Mail this coupon today!